Read other books by award-winning author, Swiyyah Woodard.
Visit www.dontcallmecrazy.com

The sequel to this book is now available! Buy now!

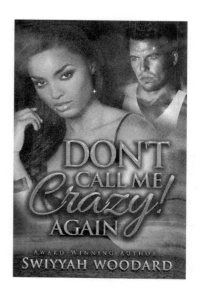

Don't Call Me Crazy! I'm Just in Love

SWIYYAH WOODARD

TABLE OF CONTENTS

CHAPTER ONE BOREDOM

The time is 3:00 a.m. Anika dreams of black pearl surroundings, a flash of white light, the sun, moon, and planets charging towards her. Is this a dream; a nightmare? She quivers with icy cold fear and awakens out of her deep slumber. She looks at her clock, turns on her light, glances at her watch and says with a tone of distress, "Damn!" She springs up like a chicken with its head cut off and grabs a few articles of clothing. Dressing quickly, she leaves, slamming the door behind her. She steps into her 1985 lackluster blue-black Ford to embark on a long journey to see Mosi, the love of her life. The man who she one day hopes to marry. An eternity can pass and she will still be waiting, ring finger pointed, for his hand in marriage.

Performing her daily ritual, Anika buckles her seat belt, starts her engine, and puts in her music, the music that makes her feel at home, the music that makes her feel love for herself and others. The joy of music is what holds her together, it's what gives her the stamina to struggle through life's trials and tribulations. She can now drive, for she has found that right song for that right moment. Amidst nightfall throttled by chalked fog, she observes American flags swaying from pole to pole, grounded outside of each store front, lining the streets.

Her eyes step past bravery crimson and glance at the purity of a royal sky filled with opal stars; which to her, represents peace and tranquility, freedom, choice, love, honor, and the hope of fulfilling the American dream. She see's car dealerships, great buildings of grandeur; corporations.

She feels she can have anything she lays her eyes upon…anything. She is aware of how corporate America chooses to advertise; the colors they use, the words used, the symbols they use, for she wants the same material possessions that those entrepreneurs possess. She wants the beatification that she sees those entrepreneurs' wives possess. She remains content as she listens to her music. She knows there are strategic steps to take to acquire the material possessions that are wanted. She exhales, inhales, and then exhales once more. She's so confident. She can stare at anything she chooses and still drive, without losing focus. Through her car mirrors she sees everything. No need to worry. She fast forwards her CD to one of her favorite songs. This song reminds her of Him, the one; He is and has always been the one. She begins to sing a song by Brandy Norwood "He is," and repeats it over and over again.

Before she knows it, she has made it to her anticipated destination. Excitedly, Anika leaps out of her car, runs up to his door, and knocks. After the third knock, here he bolts up to the door like he's spiderman. Mosi's bare, chestnut brown, muscular chest and massive broad shoulders greet her with a wet hug. She can't help but stare as his athletic shoulders squeeze through his white tee. He is a towering, slender, well-built man. He would make any woman melt down to her knees. He's rough though; rough around the edges. He is her opposite, but it was when he first spoke to her that she knew he was the one, her one and only. He was so down to earth; an honest, faithful, loyal man who would never leave her side. She was sure of it. Anika met Mosi while she was a student in one of her business courses. He had his eye on her during the entire semester, but never said a word. He was swept away by her beauty. If it were any other time, and with any other woman, he would have approached her as if she were a jungle predator, but around Anika he remained without words. Anika had to be the one to initiate conversation. She, too, had her eyes on him until the semester's end. In the last month of classes, she realized she would have to make the first move.

It was on a Friday, she remembers, right after Christmas. She arrived ten minutes early to class, for she knew he would be the only one waiting for class to start. And she would have her opportunity to speak to him with no interference from other classmates. She gathered her uneasy nerves and spoke.

"Did you get anything good for Christmas?" Anika asked. He was startled by her voice. So much time had passed and she had never spoken a word to him before this. He swallowed and fought to utter just one word. His first words stumbled off his tongue.

"I, I had a good Christmas. I got a lot gifts. How about you?" Mosi asked. Anika was then struck with words of a player.

"I wish I would have had you for Christmas," Anika said. The ice was then broken and they began to chuckle.

Before meeting Anika, Mosi was a player. He didn't believe in being faithful to one woman. He thought monogamy was a belief held only by the insane. Handsome man that he is, women catered to him. He didn't have to lift a finger. He had one woman who would clean for him, one who would run his errands, and one who was available for sex, any time, day or night. Anika, to Mosi, is a wonder woman. She is a beautiful young Capricorn born in January and unknowingly surrounded in purple rain, which is the natural color of her aura. She has a petite seducing figure; curvy like an hour glass. Her long jet-black hair shines as it flows down her slender back and her flawless coffee skin is as beautiful and smooth as silk and satin. She is kind to a fault and is forever reaching out to those in need, which sometimes can pull her into what some people may see as, 'drama.' She portrays herself as an extremely approachable woman from the wild color selection of her clothes to the type of jewelry she wears. She's what some people may call eccentric; although people know she can be trusted and will undoubtedly solve all things through love.

Mosi smiles, his bleached snow-white teeth are lined in a row of perfection. The warmth of his smile takes her breath away, every time. Inhale, pause, exhale, pause, inhale, pause. His jaw thrust forward and he kisses her softly curled plum lips. The corners of her mouth then turns upwards, as she returns his kiss.

"So how was the long drive?" Mosi asks as his aroused pupils welcome her into his lavish home. His home looks as though it was decorated by a professional interior designer. A late renaissance canvas covers his beige walls. His ivory ceiling appears to rise with no end in sight, and his eggshell carpet feels of rabbit's fur.

"Fine, I love to drive," Anika replies. He fixes her a late-night snack. They both sit on his leather chaise and enjoy watching television on his 65-inch. Anika's eyes begin to look peaked; as she dozes off. Mosi awakens her with his sexy voice.

"You're not falling asleep already, are you?" He asks as his u-shaped grin presses up against his dimples. She does not reply, but attempts to awaken as she staggers towards the bedroom. She knows what it is he wants without nary a word spoken. Her eyes fall, pressing weight on her curled lashes.

Four hours later she awakens again, only to bathe, say her good-byes, and rush off to work. Nine to five, eight hours a day, forty hours a week and on call; year after year. Working for others bothers her. She wants her own business. She wants to be the one of power who takes charge, who gives orders, who is in control. This is what she desires. Anika day dreams as she sits on her hard computer chair, with virtually no leg room and enters nothing but numbers all day. How exciting, Anika thinks. She begins to mumble, "I can't wait until thirty years from now when I can retire and this company will finally take care of me." *Yeah right. That's unrealistic*, Anika thinks. *Most employees probably won't even last five years and definitely not ten.* She remembers a former coworker who was in her tenth year of employment and quit right before she was due to retire. This employee, without warning, was given additional job responsibilities; much more than she could handle. The subordinate did not know it then, but Anika knew that since she was earning so much from the company she worked for, after raises for ten years, the owner could no longer afford to pay her the same salary.

So instead of firing her, a sneakier plan was chosen; one that was decided by the surreptitious management team to force her into quitting. Pretty smart, Anika thinks. The time has passed today within a blink of an eye and she realizes that it's nearing 5:30 p.m. and she needs to rush off to class.

Just as Anika's feet press the floor, here comes Mr. Boss Man. His red neck reaches her sight before his face does. He's from Deep South, Mississippi; brags of being country and dresses the part to a T. Day after day he dresses in loosely worn blue jean jumpsuits that have enough pockets to hold the contents of a wallet in each one. His feet are in his heavy onyx stone shoes, teeth are tarnished straw colored, from excessive use of to-bacco and home brewed whisky. His eyes bloodshot russet, skin rugged from hard work, and his hair is reminiscent of hay. He's proud of the awards his pig receives for racing each year. Anika's anxious eyes kept a sturdy stare as he strides towards her, erect and confident. Anika's right eye peeks up at him with a look of timid surrender.

"What did I do wrong?" She whispers as sweat dribbles from her restless fingertips and lands on her quivering legs. Mr. Boss Man's eyes pause and his forehead droops in inquisition causing his eyes to squint.

"Nothing, why is it that every time I come to your desk you think you have done something wrong? I need to give you a quick evaluation. For the past two weeks you have been tardy for four days; one more day late and you could be terminated. Is there a reason for your tardiness?" Mr. Boss Man said with an aggressive look in his stern sky-blue eyes.

"Lately I haven't been able to sleep much. When I finally do go to sleep, I only have a few hours to rest and my alarm clock is not doing much good in waking me up," Anika rambles while biting down on her manicured burgundy fingernails.

"What do you think can be done to improve your attendance?" Mr. Boss Man asks as he stares into her eyes. Anika cannot look into his eyes for she is afraid he might read her mind and know that she feels guilty for her tardiness. Anika lifts her head.

"Maybe I should buy another alarm clock, one that's much louder," Anika said.

"That sounds like a good idea; just make sure you follow through," Mr. Boss Man said.

"Also I have noticed your keying errors have doubled within the last two weeks; please let's make sure you are double-checking your data entry before you turn it in. Other than that, you are doing great. I know you're anxious to leave, so you have a nice day," Mr. Boss Man says.

Anika then releases the breath that her diaphragm was holding, grabs her book bag, and surges off to her economics class.

She is taking classes in business administration and psychology at the top business University in the nation, the University of South Florida. Several of her professors work for the President of the United States; because of this, she feels privileged to be a student. Even though she fails some of her difficult tests, she remains proud. Through going to college part-time throughout the years, Anika has learned a great deal about marketing, economics, management, accounting, finance, and just about anything anyone would need to know about psychology.

Her most challenging class is "Womanist Vision in Religion." This class is not challenging because of the subject itself. It is only challenging because she has to squeeze in time out of her day to write papers. She's required to write papers on topics ranging from racism to religion; the sort of topics you dare only to discuss with a select few. She has a voluminous amount of knowledge on a variety of subjects coupled with the ability to effectively communicate with others. She is a natural tutor and teacher. She wants to teach those who have an open mind and are ready to learn.

Sometimes she feels as if her mind will explode sending pieces of knowledge to those of want and need. She has learned from her mother to always have an open mind and always be ready to shut up and listen because as her mother says, 'You just might learn something.' She's always so busy thinking she sometimes has an arduous time focusing in her classes. Her economics teacher startles her when he speaks louder to get the attention of those who loaf in his class. This professor misses nothing; his eyes are perfectly glued to the back of his head. He has been in the teaching profession for ten years, is brilliant and quite wealthy. His tailor-made, midnight black suits possess an air of intimidation and creates an illusion of height. A day doesn't pass where he forgets to mention that which is valuable to him, namely his shiny, black, voice activated and responsive Lexus, while adorning his uneven toupee.

"Ms. Muhammad, are we daydreaming again?" Professor Sharks says as the lines across his forehead squeeze tight and his eyebrows droop into a downward slope.

"No, sir. I am definitely paying attention, sir; you were speaking about poverty and how only one percent of America's households makes one hundred grand or more," Anika says as her eyes remain shut.

"That's correct. Please try to focus more in class please," Professor Sharks says. Before she knows it, her economics class is over and she hurries off to her next class, Womanist Vision in Religion. How boring it is to listen to this instructor, Anika thinks. But she does because her gut tells her that this teacher has something important to teach. A six-foot tall omnipotent African-American woman stands in front of the chalkboard. Her braided black hair is covered in a dark sateen wrap; African print covers her elongated dress.

"Does anyone here agree with many theologians who feel that they have been oppressed by a patriarchal society?" Mrs. Kadeem asks, standing erect.

Anika slowly raises her hand. "Yes, I agree. I think some people interpret and use religion as a means to control others," Anika answers in stuttered speech.

"May I ask what religion you choose to study?" Mrs. Kadeem asks, lifting her chin upward.

"I am not a part of any religious organization," Anika replies.

"Well, class, throughout this semester these essays will make you think; they just may develop you spiritually. And you will learn how many theologians view religion. After viewing this film that I am about to show, your assignment will be to write an essay describing how Mahalia Jackson contributed to Christianity." Anika has completed the first essay required of the class and she briefly reads over her work before turning it in.

CHAPTER 2 DEPRESSION

One of Anika's best friends, Mary, gives her a call while she is driving home. Mary is first in line for the drama queen award. If there is not drama in her life, she will make it her responsibility to create it. If drama moves out of her life, she will surely follow, and if her friends are lacking drama, she will definitely give a helping hand. Mary has been Anika's best friend for six years. She is what most would call a hoochie. She wears large earrings that stretch her earlobes, her four-inch long rainbow bright nails angle into sharp edged shapes that she paints to match her toes. The dirt on her three inch heels outline the pattern of her feet and her legs have never been shaved. Somehow, Mary thinks this will attract men. Not only that, but her hair is braided thickly with 100% horse hair and reaches past her waist. She wears skintight clothing to attract men. She goes through more men in one month than most do in a lifetime and somehow this makes Mary think she's an expert at relationships. The phone rings and Anika answers it, "Hello?"

"Hey, what's up girl? Whatcha up to?" Mary asks.

"Nothing much, Mary; I'm just coming from class. How about you?" Anika replies.

"I'm not doing much. I got a favor though," Mary says with insecurity in her voice.

"I need a ride to HH Kencler. Can you give me a ride?"

"Sure, when do you want me to pick you up?"

"As soon as you get a chance," Mary says.

"All right then, I'm on my way," Anika says.

"All right; see you later," replies Mary.

Anika then begins her drive over to Mary's home. Mary is waiting outside Bethel Heights with a few male friends when Anika drives up. Music from several apartments is blasting loudly. There's a smell of marijuana in the air. Children are playing tag through the brown grass and several young men rest across their neighbor's cars talking about how much money they plan to make.

"Hey, what's up, girl? I'm glad you got here so soon. I can always depend on you," Mary says beaming.

"So how's everything going? How are you and your lover man? Are y'all doing all right?" Mary asks.

"We're doing OK. We have our ups and downs but we're OK," Anika says.

"So you and him working things out again, huh? I can't believe you still with him after all that. I would have been left him. First he cheats on you, then he leaves you for another woman, then he kicks you out of his apartment. What's next? How long have y'all have been going together, anyway?"

"Eight years," Anika says. Mary and her male friends burst out in uncontrollable cackling causing Anika to feel self--conscious. They all screeched out, "Eight years!"

"You for real? I would have left him. You should leave him. He ain't nothing! He should have never done those things to you," Mary says with a look of repulsion across her face.

"After one year you should know whether or not a man's good enough to marry. Eight years? He's just using you for sex," Brian says as he pulls up his sagging pants and passes the rolled up marijuana joint.

"Somebody that looks as good as you, I would have been married. It don't take no eight years to know if you the right one," Reggie says.

"Yeah, you're right. But I'm not going to leave him," Anika says as she folds her arms in a poised manor. Mary sees the grief on her face.

"You know I'm only trying to help you right?" Mary says. Anika replies, "Yeah I know."

"See, it's like this. When a man ain't doing what he's supposed to be doing, you got to put him in his place. You want to get married, right?" Mary asks.

"Yeah," Anika replies.

"Well," Mary says, "you're not getting any younger; you got to put your foot down and tell him he better marry you because you have been with him for eight years; eight long years and you're tired of this mess. If you're thinking of staying with him, y'all might as well get married. You can have anybody you want and you know that. You are young, attractive, and smart. Forget him. All he's going to do is cheat on you again. Once a cheat, always a cheat," Mary says while slapping her outer thighs.

"He may not cheat again. And I never actually caught him cheating; I just suspected that he was a cheater," Anika says.

"You got that right; he may not cheat again, but chances are that he will, and you are worth more than that.

You got to find your worth. You don't have any confidence in yourself; that's the problem. You got to start standing up for yourself more. You got to get some male balls," Mary says.

"Some what?" Anika says. "Some balls?" Mary says.

"All right, I think I get the point!" Anika says as the palm of her right hand pushes the air.

"It sounds like you're contradicting yourself. First you say I need to leave him then you say I need to marry him. What are you trying to say?" Anika asks.

"I'm not offending you, am I? I'm sorry if I am; I was just speaking the truth. You crazy if you stay with him," Mary says as her eyes roll in a disrespectful manner.

"I am not crazy; I love that man. I don't care what any of you say I want to marry him and he will marry me one day," Anika says.

"Sure he will," Brian and Reggie say while laughing and hitting their hands together. Anika and Mary step into the Ford. They both remain quiet as they pull up to the store. They're quiet the entire time while shopping. After Mary is done shopping, Anika drops her off and they say their good-byes.

Anika's now on her way to her mother's house. She is feeling down as a result of the conversation with Mary and her friends. She searches different radio stations for that right song that will calm her shaken nerves. Her fingers halt at 95.7, the beat with Steve Harvey. She arrives at her mother's house and immediately begins telling her mother how upset she is and fills her in on the details of what just happened.

Her mother wears a beautiful lilac scarf covering her natural ebony hair. Her dress flows down touching her ankles. The ankle bracelet and toe ring is the only means in which to show off her sexuality. Ms. Muhammad has gone through more tragedy in life than most. Her first husband was abusive; Anika's father. He always accused her of infidelity. When she would arrive home from work, he would check her underwear for signs of cheating. Besides going to work, she could not leave his side. He would verbally abuse and demean her.

"You got to be smarter than a paper bag," he would say. The first day that he struck her was when she was returning from her sister's birthday party. It was past two and he accused her of spending the night with another man. She raised her voice for the first time, to defend her honor and prove her innocence, but before she could utter another sound, the back of his right hand flew through the air and landed across her cheek.

From that point on, she made plans to live a life on her own. She opened a separate bank account without his knowledge. The funds were automatically drafted from her pay every two weeks. Once she had enough money for her own apartment, she planned to flee. She underestimated her husband's inquisitive nature and on the day of escape, he shot her seven times. Thank God she survived. She had other misfortunes throughout her life. She's lost three jobs, two homes, two cars, four husbands, and was involved in two fatal car accidents. Life has been challenging for Ms. Muhammad, but she never gives up. She has an A and C personality. She's high-strung, yet will attempt to please others to the point of self-sacrifice.

"Mom, I'm so upset and embarrassed. Mary made me look like a fool in front of her friends, telling them how I've been with Mosi for eight years and telling me that I should dump him. I'm not going to listen to her advice, I love that man," Anika says. Her mother sits up straight in her seat.

"You must know who you are and your purpose in life so you will not be so affected by what others say. You must learn how to solve your own problems. One of the reasons I don't give advice is because it might come back to bite you if it's not what they want to hear. Besides, most people want you to just listen to them when they have a problem instead of telling them what to do. And, I try to stay away from drama at all cost."

"What do you mean, drama?" Anika questions with a perplexed look on her face trying to fit the puzzle pieces of Ms. Muhammad's teaching.

"Drama," the mother explains, "is characterized by a lot of things. Number one, just as in your situation, when everything is going well, a person enjoys digging up past pains and traumas in order to have for themselves a dramatic excitable conversation. The friend may feel as if they are helping you come to the right decision, even though only you are the only one who can make the right decisions for you. Number two, pay attention to who your friends are and which family members you get along with best. Nine times out of ten, we choose to surround ourselves around people that compliment us. If we want drama, we hang around negative individuals; if we want happiness and success, we hang around positive people.

Think about it. Number three, sometimes when we have a fear of making our own decisions we push others into making decisions for us. An example being, if a person asks how you are doing, say, 'I am doing just fine.' If they ask how you are doing and your reply is to tell them every last bad thing that has happen to you within the last week, that gives the drama-stricken people the opportunity to engage in negativity. You want to stay away from negativity at all cost. I don't even watch dramatic programs on television; shoot, I don't even watch the depressing daily news. Negativity and the inability to solve your own problems as an adult, sometimes bring about depression. We all experience depression at one time or another, but some people experience it all the time and if that's the case, they must ask themselves why it occurs."

"Well, I'm always depressed and I need to know why," Anika says. Anika's mother offers advice, "Depression for me, comes from a lack of freedom. I'd like to be free to utilize my natural- born talents to engage in activities that help others, but I'm too busy working nine to five. The secret is to work full-time for as long as it takes you to save money to start a business, and utilize your talents to help others. You have to set goals and visualize yourself reaching them. Share your goals only with people who want to see you succeed. Taking risks is a part of becoming the person you want to be, Anika."

"That makes a lot of sense," her mother's daughter sits attentively, focusing on the knowledge imparted to her.

21

Anika's mother continues, "Depression also stems from stress and the inability to control your life. You have to be in control of your own life and be able to face life head on. Some people run to the bottle or drugs when a problem arises; they drink or smoke, but once they come down from their high they're faced with the same problems. It's best to just face life and find ways to jump over those obstacles that we face. Know that we are tested daily and have the tools necessary to rise above it all. Learn to love life, Anika. Love the fight, love the small things that we are blessed to have and experience. Love yourself. This is how to develop spiritually," Anika's mother says with confidence.

"I do agree, but we are learning in class that a person who is depressed may have a chemical imbalance in their brain," Anika says.

"This is true; you're speaking mainly about clinical depression. There can definitely be a chemical imbalance that will cause this disorder," Ms. Muhammad says. While in middle of conversation, another friend calls Anika. It's Rachel, who is second in line for the drama queen award. Gossip and drama strike again! Rachel is best friends with Mary and she's Anika's associate. She acts as if she worships Mary. She's always following Mary's footsteps. If Mary doesn't like a new boyfriend of Rachel's, Rachel will find an excuse to rid herself of him. Rachel feels Mary's advice is always spot on. Rachel moved from a small city when she was young and never made too many friends while in school. Everyone saw her as stuck-up and selfish. Even her own mother celebrated the day she left home. She talks with a southern Ebonics accent and carries herself like the Queen of England.

Her ears are green from her CZ diamonds she wears and she has faded gold rings on each finger. Her clothing is cheap, never costing more than ten dollars per garment. Her life is so dull and lonely that whenever Mary brings up drama, Rachel welcomes it with open arms.

"What's up," says Rachel. Anika replies, "Nothing much."

"I heard yah havin' problems with yah boyfriend," Rachel says.

"Who told you that?" Anika says with an astounded expression on her face.

"Oh, I was just talkin' to Mary and she says that you were unhappy because things were not goin' as well as you want them to go," Rachel says.

"That is not true. Everything between me and Mosi are OK. We have our ups and downs but we are working things out," Anika says while biting down on her burgundy lips in frustration.

"Well, how long are y'all two goin' to work things out? Gosh, to me it seems like you two are always havin' so many ups and downs. And I'm only saying this because I care about you and I think you should have the best and if he is not the best, then you know what you need to do. You need to leave him if he keeps disrespecting you," Rachel says.

"Well, I'm getting sick and tired of every one telling me what I need to do about my man," Anika says.

"The only reason everyone is tellin' you what you need to do is because they care about you and they are tired of seein' you get hurt. Shoot. You should have the best, like I say, you should never settle."

"Well, it seems to me that all of my friends are single, so how can someone who is single tell me what to do with my man," Anika says.

"Because we all have experience with no-good men; you are new to this. And we don't want you to go through the same things that we had to go through," Rachel says.

"Well, maybe everyone should leave me alone and let me live my own life," Anika says. Rachel gets offended at Anika's retort and shouts out, "Fine. I was just trying to help you." Then she hangs up the receiver without saying good-bye.

At that point, Anika is baffled and feels as if she can't please anyone. She goes into the other room and begins to cry. It felt to her that a thunderstorm of rain was showering down her cheeks and throughout her heart. Her mother is very aware of what's going on, but says nothing. She wants Anika to work things out on her own, like a true adult. It is her belief that once a person reaches the point in their life where they are able to learn from their own mistakes they have become a true adult and should take responsibility for their own actions. Anika, after crying her eyes out, calls upon the love of her life; her boyfriend, Mosi.

"Hey, what's up? Whatcha up to?" Anika asks. Mosi replies, "I'm just watching television. How about yourself?"

"Oh, I'm not doing much," Anika says. "I'm kinda upset though."

"Oh yeah, what's up?" Mosi.

"Well, my friend was saying how I take a lot of mess from you and that I need to leave you alone," Anika says.

"Well, why are you listening to your friends?" Mosi becomes aggravated.

"I'm not," Anika replies.

"Well, then, end of discussion," Mosi says.

"Are you coming over tonight, you know I'm going to throw something on the grill?" Mosi asks.

"Yeah, I might; depending on how I feel, but right now I'm going to take a nap, so I'll call you later," Anika says. They say their good-byes and she drifts off to sleep. Mosi decides to meet up with his former friends from college at a local dance club. His friends are what he used to be, but that's no surprise since we all hang around those who are most similar to us.

Tony is Mosi's closest friend and is pure trouble. He's the type who is disrespectful towards women. He used to date Mary back in the day, but she cut him off after receiving a call from one of his women. All women should obey him, no questions asked. Beige wife-beaters, Timberland boots and pant housing are basically his uniform and he proudly displays his two carat diamond earring in his right ear. A pretty boy, plain and simple, he's nothing but a thug. Inside the bar are their other old buddies, Richard and Mike.

"Hey, what's up, man. I haven't seen you in a while. What have you been up to?" Tony asks as he slaps Mosi on the back.

"Nothing much just into the same things," Mosi says.

"Oh yeah, and what's that; liquor and women." Tony's smile reaches both of his ears.

"No way. I'm a one-woman man now. I don't have the time nor want to fool around," Mosi says.

"Yeah, sure, I haven't seen the other guys yet, let's go inside, maybe they're in there waiting for us," Tony says. Richard is preppy to say the least; always neatly dressed with his polo shirts tucked into his Dickies. Richard loves the ladies but can't keep a girlfriend to save his life. He tries to be a player but falls short every time and knows nothing about women. Raised by his father who suffered from six divorces, he takes no responsibility for his relationships failing. You would think that by him being a heart surgeon, women would be flocking toward him, but that's simply not the case. They both enter the club and see Richard and Mike standing up against the wall holding beers and scoping out the women from one end of the establishment to the other.

"It is so good to see you, man. I miss hanging out with a real player," Richard says.

"Not anymore. I'm staying loyal to my woman," Mosi says.

"What woman? What's her name?" Richard and the other guys tightly press their hands up against their mouths in order to hold back their obviously jealous laughter.

"I'm seeing the same woman I've been seeing for the past eight years," Mosi says with agitation.

"You can't just let a beautiful woman go, can you?"

"You can be honest with us, we're your boys. Who else are you seeing?" Tony insists.

"I'm being honest. I'm a changed man. Love changed me," Mosi says. Now, Mike is a ladies' man. He knows how to treat a woman; making each of them feel like they are the only one. Because of his attentive demeanor he finds himself attracting primarily older women. They love his shapely beard and his dark brown complexion. The long-time friends make their way to the bar.

"You can't expect us to believe that one, after all the wrong you have done to that woman. Can you?" Tony asks.

"What? I've always been faithful to her. Yes, I used to be a player, but that's when I was a boy; now I'm a man. I have different needs right now in my life. I'm even thinking about marrying her," Mosi says.

"Marriage! Don't do it. Man, your whole life will be a ball and chain. You can forget about your freedom. Can you imagine only being with one woman for the rest of your life? Why punish yourself? One of us needs to snap you back into reality," Mike says leaning back in his chair.

"What do you know about marriage, are you married?" Mosi says.

"Hell no!" Mike shouts.

"Then why would I care to take your advice on something you know absolutely nothing about?" Mosi challenges.

"Mike has a point. Do your research. Fifty percent of all marriages end in divorce. Be smart about it," Tony says.

"I am thinking smart. Why do most marriages end in divorce? It's because of financial difficulty. I will have my own separate bank account and so will she. I will spend my money the way I choose and so will she," Mosi says.

"It's not that simple, my friend. Everything must be joint, including bank accounts. Face it, there's no way to escape the inevitable; you two will not make it," Tony says.

"I've been with this woman for eight years, do you really think that marriage would cause us to break up? What you guys don't realize is that the true marriage is in the commitment. If you can't be committed to your women before marriage, how in the world do you expect to be committed once the ring is on your finger? Your history will only repeat itself," Mosi says.

"Uh-huh. Face reality," Tony says sarcastically.

"You know, he might be right; no one should judge their relationship, and it just might work," Richard says.

"Well, I don't think so. Look at all of these beautiful women. Look at that one over there on the dance floor. I think she is eyeing you, man. What are you going to do? Don't disappoint me," Tony says.

"I told you. I'm faithful. You can feel free to talk to her," Mosi says.

"But she is eyeing you and look, she's walking this way. What are you going to do, man, don't disappoint us," Tony says. The woman then saunters over to Mosi. Her demanding legs angle down from her polyester mini skirt as she sits on his lap. This woman is beautiful. She is Caucasian with a golden tan. Her curly, honey-blond hair falls between her bosoms. Her lips are plum-red and she has cheeks of cherry.

"You're kinda cute. What's your name?" the woman asks. "I'm taken." Mosi says. The guys then begin to holler, "He's not taken, he doesn't know what he is saying. I think he had too much to drink!"

"What's your name, sweet thing?" Mike asks.

"My name is Sexy, but I'm not interested in you. I'm interested in your friend here." Just as Sexy begins to get up from Mosi's lap, in marches Mary and her gossiping friend Rachel.

"Did you see that? Did you see what I just saw?

"That woman was sittin' on his lap. I told you. I told you he wasn't no good. Now what are you gonna do? Anika is your best friend. Are you going to tell her or what?" Rachel says.

"No. There's no need to jump to conclusions," Mary says.

"No need, that woman was sittin' on his lap. How do you explain that? There's no explanation. He was trying to hit on her. I told you. I told you he could not be trusted," Rachel says.

"You might just be right," Mary says. Mary and Rachel tread across the floor over to Mosi. Tony spots them first.

"Look who's walking this way. Ain't that Mary and Rachel? I used to date her. Mary is crazy. What do they want?" Tony says. Mary takes measures into her own hands, throws back her right arm, grabs a hand full of air, plunges forward and across Mosi's face.

"What the hell do you think you are doing?" A burning look of hate strikes his eyes as he clenches his teeth.

"My girlfriend's at home by herself and here you are hoeing round. You should be ashamed of yourself," Mary says, as she shakes her right index finger in a motion of blame. He jumps up and gets in her face.

"What in the hell do you think you're doing?" Mosi says as a flared rage of anger reverberates throughout his speech.

"I saw you and I saw that woman on your lap. You ain't nothin' but a cheat and I'm telling Anika," Mary says.

"What are you talking about, you crazy girl? Get out of my face," Mosi says. He then walks off, holding his jaw in shame.

"I see you just as crazy as you have always been," Tony says.

"Shut up," Mary says as she turns her back and exits the club with Rachel.

"What are you gonna do? Are you gonna tell her or what?" Rachel asks.

Mary then phones Anika.

"I'm sorry to tell you this, but your boyfriend is at the club picking up other women," Mary says.

"I just spoke to him a few hours ago, he is not at the club," Anika says with curiosity.

"Yes he is. I saw it with my own two eyes; another woman sitting on his lap. Rachel saw it, too. I wouldn't lie to you. Come out to the club, you'll see," Mary says.

"You mean to tell me that my man is cheating on me? I can't believe that!" Anika's words collided against the receiver.

"Believe it. I'm sorry, but it's true. You need to come out here," Mary says.

"Out where?" Anika asks.

"To the same club we always go to, silly. Club Karma on First Avenue South and Eighteenth Street," Mary says. Anika then grabs her car keys and heads out the door. She calls her boyfriend while she is driving but he does not answer. She mumbles underneath her breath while she is driving.

"He better not be cheating on me. After all that we have been through, and he would have the nerve to cheat. Oh no; not my man. I can't believe him. Wait until I get there. I'm going to tell him off in front of everyone. Why would he do this to me?" Tears begin to pool in her eyes as she begins to cry. "I've given him eight years of my life, I thought he changed. He had me fooled. Right underneath my nose and I didn't even smell it. This is it; it's over. I'm not taking any more mess from him. I thought we were becoming closer. Ha! Boy, was I wrong.

That conniving snake, inviting me to come over to his house for some barbecue and he's up in some club while I'm home; the nerve of him. He did not tell me about going to no club. Wait until I get there. I'm going to give him a piece of my mind. Thank God for my friends; without them I would be lost. Lost like a naive little girl. Yeah, he played me; he played me for a fool. But not anymore, it's all over. He can play around with some other woman. I'm strong now. I don't need him. I can do bad all by myself. He ain't all that anyway. Walking around with his nose up in the air like he's the King of England. He ain't nobody. Think he can get away with cheating on me. He's crazy. Wait until I get there."

When she pulls up to the club she sees Mosi and his friends heading for their cars. The dirt on the ground from which she walks scurries away from her barging feet, as she stumps over to Mosi. The guys are all laughing and Mary and Rachel stand there cheering her on.

"I can't believe you; I can't believe you would do this to me!" Anika's pounding heart is felt by Mosi as he clutches onto her arm and walks her over to her car.

"Go home and I will call you. You're making a fool out of yourself," Mosi says. Anika then begins to drive home and calls Mosi on the way.

"Why, why, how can you do this to me? I love you so much. How can you be at the club flirting with women, allowing them to sit on your lap like you're some baller? Mary told me. She told me everything," Anika says as her frown lines deepen and her anxiety grows into panic.

"Mary told you what? Mary did not see me do anything. You're acting paranoid. You always think I'm cheating on you when I'm not. You're always are so paranoid," Mosi says.

"Don't you dare call me crazy. You're crazy for risking an eight year relationship for some tramp," Anika says.

"What are you talking about? I've done nothing wrong. You need to check your friends," Mosi says.

"Oh, you've done something wrong. How come you did not answer your phone when I called you? Tell me that," Anika says.

"I left my phone in the car," Mosi says.

"Yeah right. Sure. Like I'm really supposed to believe that one. Come up with something better than that, liar," Anika says.

"I am not a liar. I'm being honest with you. Nothing happened at the club. You're acting paranoid," Mosi says.

"Well, I don't believe you. My friends would not lie to me. They're honest," Anika says.

"And I'm not?" Mosi questions.

"No, you're not," Anika demands.

"This is enough. When you calm down you give me a call," Mosi says. He hangs up the phone and Anika calls Mary.

"Are you sure you saw him with another woman?" Anika questions.

"Yes, I'm sure. And I would not lie to you," Mary says.

"How long were they together?" Anika asks.

"I don't know, as soon as we walked in, the girl got up from his lap and walked off," Mary says.

"I think he is telling the truth. I don't think he was with anyone," Anika says.

"I saw it with my own eyes. Me and Rachel did. But believe in what you want to believe in; be a sucker. I was just trying to look out for you," Mary says as her right nostril lifts in disgust.

"We will talk about this later. I'm tired and stressed and I'm going to go back to sleep now," Anika says. Anika drifts off to sleep leaving the day behind her.

CHAPTER 3 THE OTHER MAN

Anika awakens at 2:00 a.m. and realizes she has not purchased the materials needed for economics class, so she rushes out to the crowded 24-hour store. While shopping Anika accidentally bumps into a white man who was quite handsome.

"This gorgeous man would make any women sweat," Anika thinks. He is six feet tall, dressed in corporate silvery slacks, button-down silk shirt and smells of sweet obsession. His nutmeg hair is greased down, parted on the left side and hands are immense. Just one of his palms can cup a woman's bosom. Anika then reminds herself that she is a taken woman and quickly walks off. He too noticed her in the same light and being a curious man, he felt the need to introduce himself. And so he did.

"Hello my name is David and yours?" he inquires as his eyes travel outlining her curves with optimistic expectations. Anika replies quickly, "I'm a taken woman."

"I just asked your name, not your hand in marriage." Anika senses the lust in his voice and again she tries to walk away.

"Well, it was nice meeting you but I have to finish my shopping, it is kinda late," Anika says. David smiles, stares, and allows her to walk off. He is confident that if he leaves his number with the cashier to give to Anika, she will surely call. David is right because she does that same night and he answers the phone.

"Hello," David says.

"Hi, it's me. I just met you an hour ago at the 24-"

He cuts her off. "I know who this is. It's my future wife.

"What took you so long to call?" David asks.

"Oh, I wouldn't take it that far now. I just called because I was curious to know where you're from because it doesn't seem like you're from St. Petersburg. It looks like you're from somewhere like Hollywood. Are you?" Anika asks.

"Oh no, beautiful, I'm from New York, but thanks for the compliment; and yourself?" David says.

"I was born and raised here in St. Petersburg," Anika says. David cuts her off again.

"Tell me about what type of person you are. What do you want from a man? What are your likes and dislikes?" David asks.

"Well," she replies, "I was always taught not to tell a man my likes and dislikes, but to show him through my actions."

"Well, let me tell you about myself. I have been a professional singer and actor for three years now. I just recently moved here to try and find modeling work in Tampa and be closer to friends. I think I'm a nice, young, handsome man who is always trying to set goals for myself. I'll be successful one day because I'm persistent. Once I set a goal, I accomplish it regardless of the hurdles that appear before me. Now, I gave a little, so you can tell a little about yourself," David says.

"There's not much to tell. I work for—" He interrupts her again.

"You say you have someone. How serious is your relationship? I mean, are you able to have at least a friend?" David asks.

"Well, I don't believe in having a male friend. I think eventually if you spend too much time with that person, something will happen. So, I really don't have any male friends. And as far as my relationship is concerned, we are doing just fine," Anika says.

"All right that's a good enough answer. So what religion are you?"

"I really don't like to discuss religion because some people-" David cuts her off again.

"It's OK, I'm not judgmental and I have an open mind so feel free to discuss anything with me, beautiful," David says. Anika begins to ramble.

"Well, I was born into Islam as a Muslim, but my boyfriend is Baptist and so is his mother. Sometimes I go to church with them, but I really don't feel comfortable. I'm still searching for the right answers," Anika says.

"At least you're searching," David says.

"Yes I am," Anika says.

"Well, what does your heart tell you to do?" David asks.

"What do you mean?" Anika asks.

"What religion do you feel is best for you?" David asks.

"I never had anyone ask that question before." Her eyes catch the floor with a look of shame.

"To be honest with you, I really don't know. I believe in God and I believe that it really doesn't matter what religion you are as long as that religion makes you a better person and guides you closer to God. I think God is looking down on us all and asking his angels, 'Why are my children fighting over me like this. I love them all,'" Anika says.

"Well, that sounds like a good answer," David says.

"What religion are you?" Anika asks.

"I am Baptist," David says.

"Oh you, too," Anika says.

"Yes," David says.

"There's a lot I don't understand from that religion," Anika says.

"What is it that you don't understand?" David asks.

"I'd rather not talk about it. I do my own research to find out certain things about religion," Anika says.

"Well, you never have to feel afraid to ask me anything," David says.

"It's not that I'm afraid, it's just that I have an understanding that in any religion there may always be a person that is misinterpreting the Bible or the Qur'an so I am very careful as to who I go to for certain answers to certain questions," Anika says. David's head jerks backwards in offense.

"Well, I hate to end this conversation so quickly, beautiful, but it's my bedtime so I'll speak to you at another time. One love."

Anika says her good-byes and drifts off to sleep forgetting to call her boyfriend. This now stirs up a suspicious jealousy in Mosi. She calls him each night, religiously. Mosi gives her a call at 3:00 in the morning, awakening her out of her deep slumber.

"What's going on? You forgot to call me?" Mosi asks.

"I'm so sorry. I was just so tired. I fell asleep as soon as I got home. I apologize for accusing you of cheating; that was wrong of me. It won't happen again," Anika says.

"You always think I'm cheating. You don't trust me. Usually when a person is so quick to accuse another of cheating that means they are guilty of cheating themselves," Mosi says.

"What? Do you think I have a reason to cheat?" Anika asks, startled by his erroneous words.

"No, that's not what I'm saying. Don't put words in my mouth. I'm saying that if you don't trust me maybe we should not be together. You're always so suspicious. Sometimes I think you may have a mental disorder," Mosi says.

"Don't you call me crazy. You're always calling me crazy." Anika begins to raise her voice.

"If you don't want to be with me just say so. If it's another woman, let me know. Be a man!" Anika says. A sudden feeling of rage strikes Mosi's heart causing it to beat with vast velocity.

"There is no other woman; how many times do I have to tell you this. What's wrong with you?"

"There's nothing wrong with me," Anika says.

"I love you and I don't want to lose you, but you have to stop allowing your friends to put those ideas in your head. Without trust we have no relationship," Mosi says. Anika falls silent and calms down.

"I don't want to lose you either. We can talk more about this tomorrow. I really do need to rest. It has been hard for me to sleep lately. I am so sorry for not trusting you. I promise things will change." Anika then drifts off to sleep.

The week passes and it's now Sunday. David calls to invite Anika to church. She accepts. This church is massive and immaculate in Anika's eyes. She is really impressed by the amethyst painted octagon windows and the six-foot bronze statue of Jesus nailed to the cross that rests up against the moonstone walls. The church is two stories high. Anika and David sit on the balcony seats overlooking the church members as they accept the calming scent of lilac wax that slowly wafts in their direction. Anika is astounded by the amount of money that is being collected. There are tithes given for the church, for the absent preacher and the visiting preacher. The visiting preacher has a look of wealth. He's adorned in the finest linens. Anika can't help but stare at his ten carat jade diamond blinding her sight.

"I'm reading from Matthew 28:1-10. 'In the end of the Sabbath, as it began to dawn toward the first day of the week, came Mary Magdalene and the other Mary to see the sepulcher. And, behold, there was a great earthquake: for the angel of the Lord descended from heaven, and came and rolled back the stone from the door, and sat upon it. His countenance was like lightning, and his raiment white as snow: And for fear of him the keepers did shake, and became as dead men. And the angel answered and says unto the women, Fear not ye: for I know that ye seek Jesus, which was crucified. He is not here: for he is risen, as he says. Come, see the place where the Lord lay. And go quickly, and tell his disciples that he is risen from the dead; and, behold, he goeth before you into Galilee; there shall ye see him: lo, I have told you. And they departed quickly from the sepulcher with fear and great joy; and did run to bring his disciples word.

And as they went to tell his disciples, behold, Jesus met them, saying. All hail. And they came and held him by the feet, and worshipped him. Then says Jesus unto them, Be not afraid: go tell my brethren that they go into Galilee, and there shall they see me.'

"Is there anyone here today who would like to come to be saved?" Several people rise to be baptized. A few members of the church turn and look at Anika.

"What do you think? Do you want to be saved?" David asks.

"I'm not ready yet," Anika whispers.

"When you are ready, let me know I will then bring you back to church," David says.

"I just have so many questions and so much confusion about different religious denominations," Anika whispers.

"What does your heart tell you to do?" David asks.

"I don't know," Anika replies. Ms. Simpson, the oldest member of the church, turns and taps Anika on the shoulder. Her large royal blue brimmed hat scratches Anika's cheeks as she turns.

"Aren't you going to get saved today, young lady?" Ms. Simpson whispers.

"No, not today. I'm not ready," Anika says.

"What's your name?" Ms. Simpson asks with curiosity.

"Anika Muhammad."

"Muhammad! Are you a Mooslim?" Ms. Simpson's brows frown in disbelief.

"I was raised Muslim," Anika says.

"You're Mooslim, you're going to hell," Ms. Simpson says.

40

David then interrupts.

"Ms. Simpson! I can't believe you just said that," David says appalled by Ms. Simpson's disrespecting words. Ms. Simpson does not respond. She turns her back on the both of them and begins whispering to another elderly woman who sits next to her.

"If you want to leave now I will definitely understand," David says. Anika looks over to him with a look of hurt and shame. She excuses herself and walks over to the bathroom. She stares into the mirror and watches as tears creep from her right eye down the side of her right nostril and up onto her upper lip. Anika walks up to David and places her hand on his shoulder and whispers in his ear.

"I'm ready to go," Anika says. She catches Ms. Simpson's eyes staring at her long ankle skirt and closed shoes. David and Anika walk out of the church.

"I apologize for Ms. Simpson's behavior. Some members of this church have a habit of judging others."

"You don't have to apologize for her ignorance," Anika says. While driving home, Anika receives a call from her boyfriend.

"I've been calling all day, where have you been?" Mosi asks. "I went to church with a friend," Anika replies.

"You went to church! Oh my God, what made you go to church?" Mosi asks.

"I don't know, lately I'm just feeling like I need to become closer to God," Anika says.

"I'm proud of you. Did you learn anything?" Mosi asks.

"Yes, I learned a little about the Baptist religion. It was a nice experience," Anika says.

"Well, whenever you want to go to church with me just let me know. Hey, I rented a scary movie. Would you like to come over and see it?" Mosi asks.

"I think not. I don't like scary movies. I don't want to go to bed having nightmares," Anika says.

"No you won't. I'll explain the movie to you. Come on over," Mosi says. Anika then drives over to her boyfriend's apartment. All the lights are off and the candles are lit. Mosi sits there in the middle of the living room floor watching the movie.

"You left your door open," Anika says.

"I know. Come and sit and watch Mothman Prophecies. You just might learn something," Mosi says.

"So what is this movie really about?" Anika asks.

"It's about psychics. People who can see future disasters," Mosi answered.

"Do you really believe in this stuff?" Anika asks.

"Yes, notice that a few of the characters in this movie are hearing voices. Those voices that they are hearing are really two things, their spiritual guides or spirits, warning them about future events," Mosi says.

"That's not true, they're hearing voices because they are schizophrenic," Anika says.

"No, that's not always true. Aren't you the one that does not believe in the word crazy?" Mosi asks.

"Yes," Anika says.

"Well, listen and let me explain. This movie is showing that some people who are diagnosed with a mental illness are not really crazy. The voices they hear in their heads are real. Sometimes the person may hear a voice clearly or may hear an annoying distorted chirping sound," Mosi says.

"And you picked all this up from watching this movie," Anika says.

"I've done my own research into the world of parapsychology. You must keep an open mind. There are a lot of unknowns in this world. Some things you may not be able to conclusively prove, like spirits, no one can prove that spirits exist, but many believe in them," Mosi says.

CHAPTER 4 BOUNDARIES

Almost two months have passed. It is now February 26, 2000, 8:15 a.m. and Anika awakens, realizing that she is late for work. She bathes, snatches on the first article of clothing she can find, and runs for the front door. Finally after a long drive she makes it to work only to see that a curly brunette is sitting in her seat. How frustrating, Anika thinks.

"Excuse me," Anika says.

"Oh, I'm sorry. Am I in your seat? Let me get up. My mistake." The new employee extends her hand for a proper introduction.

"My name is Kris and yours?" the new employee says. Anika gives a blank stare. She is so perturbed she could hardly utter a word.

"I'm sorry if I offended you, how long have you been working here?" Kris asks.

"I have been working here for a year," Anika says. "Do you enjoy this type of work?" Kris asks.

"I can't complain. It's a job, right? I'm paying my bills," Anika says.

"It seems to be that a person would get bored working at a place like this for a year and only getting paid minimum wage. I'm only here part-time. I work for a non-profit crisis unit as a therapist where I deal with people of all ages who have issues ranging from depression to mental breakdowns," Kris says.

"Do you believe that some people are insane?" Anika inquires.

"That is what the medical profession calls it. Forty-nine percent of the U.S. population will suffer from a psychiatric illness at some point in their lives. Most common are anxiety, substance abuse, and depression. That means just about everyone has at least one person in their family that will suffer from a mental disorder. I see all clients not as patients with mental illnesses, but as unhealthy people with brain chemical deficiencies. Some of my coworkers talk about the clients to their friends and family, which is highly unethical and their perception is a little different from mine."

Anika asks, "What do you mean?"

"I mean that a lot of the staff treats clients like they are inhuman. I believe that a lot of times after medication and much rest, the clients convert back to their natural self, but when the clients are treated like mentally ill patients they begin to act like crazy people," Kris says.

"I see a lot of the staff starting arguments with the clients or taking their frustrations out on the clients."

"So you are saying that it is other people that makes a person crazy?" Anika asks.

"No, that is not what I am saying. I'm saying that no one knows what causes mental illness and as a professional I must continue to observe and do research in order to find the answers.

And I have watched several clients go through a thirty-day transition. First they come in like walking zombies after being giving strong medications; medications you would give to a horse. And then just as the medication is wearing off the staff begins to treat them not as adults but as crazy lunatics and then there's the client's family. Many times they're no better. They also treat the client as if the client is a helpless adult," Kris says.

"So you feel it's the person's parents who have raised them wrong which in turn caused them to develop a mental disorder?" Anika asks.

"No, not at all. Mental illness is no one's fault. The way a person is raised may have nothing to do with whether or not they develop a mental disorder. No one knows what causes mental disorders, but I assure you a person's parents are not always to blame. Most likely, there's unbalanced brain chemistry," Kris says.

"Wow. It seems like you go through a lot on that job of yours. How is it you're able to make it through the day without quitting?" Anika asks. Kris begins to rock back and forth in her chair, anxious to give an answer.

"That's a good question. I avoid confrontation with the other employees by keeping to myself, staying observant, and staying away from negative conversations. This is how I get through the day and keep a smile on my face. This is how I keep my spirits up," says Kris.

"It seems to me that the stress from hearing all of your clients' problems can drain you dry." Anika asks.

"When I started working as a therapist I would allow clients to treat me as if I was a friend. I had not yet developed as a professional, nor did I know enough about setting boundaries," Kris says.

"What do you mean by boundaries?" Anika asks.

"Everyone has their own space; space that you do not allow anyone to come into. If someone does something or says something that you do not like, you say NO. And since I had a hard time saying no, I allowed myself to get run over. I got run over by my supervisor, by the other therapists, and by the clients. I realized that when you try to please everyone, you sacrifice your own needs. And if you come into harm, then you can't blame anyone, but yourself," Kris says.

"What do you mean you were run over by your supervisor?" Anika asks.

"Well, before I went back to school to pursue my master's degree in family counseling, I was asked to be a therapist for a non-profit program," Kris says.

"But how can you do therapy with only a BA degree?" Anika asks.

"Exactly. I was asked to do therapy; I refused, and almost lost my job."

"How were you able to keep your job?" Anika asks with a voice of curiosity.

"Well, I had to be sneaky. Instead of doing the solution- focused therapy that I was told to do, I continued to, without the supervisor knowing it, work only as a social worker. And in order for her not to find out, I had to become a genius at writing client progress notes. I was successful for a while until the supervisor caught on," Kris says.

"What are progress notes?" Anika asks.

"Progress notes are a description of the weekly progress of a client. Each time a client improved or worsened, we had to document it," Kris says.

"Well, if you did not do therapy, how did any of the clients get better?" Anika asks.

"A lot of the clients got better just because they had someone to listen to. Adults can sometimes work through their problems on their own, unless they have a severe mental disorder," Kris says.

"What did you do when one of your clients had a severe mental problem?" Anika asks.

"That happened once and I did ask for assistance from my supervisor and the therapist, but was only told that I can handle things on my own so my only solution was to refer the client to another program," Kris says.

"You mean there was a therapist working within the same program and she wouldn't help you?" Anika says with an appalling look on her face. Kris begins to show frustration.

"No, she didn't. And this is what I mean by being taking advantage of. I was manipulated by the therapist and supervisor. They both thought anyone could do therapy, even if they weren't qualified. I felt as if I was being emotionally abused. It seemed like at least twice a month I would get into arguments with the supervisor. She wouldn't take no for an answer. I think she had a mental disorder. I don't think she really had experience necessary to do the job she was hired for. She was probably promoted because she was good friends with the hiring manager. Every time we had a meeting about our pilot program she would ask the same damn question which filled up the entire meeting. What can we do to get more clients? We would reply the same way each time. We need a manager to meet with the principals of the schools in order to recruit more clients. What we were saying is that it was her damn job to recruit clients, not ours. She'd continue to badger me for answers even after the meetings," Kris begins to laugh.

"It angered me to work for this non-profit program because as you probably know, there's little funding for these programs and so managers don't hire enough staff and that puts too much responsibility on us. It made the job way too stressful for me to handle."

"One day I walked past her office and saw her on the floor and when she saw me, she jumped up. And when she was upset, she would walk down the office screaming. No lie. I remember one psychologist who was speaking about treatment for one of her clients. She was looking for a diagnosis. I heard her telling one of her coworkers that it did not matter what diagnosis she gave because the young patient was too far gone mentally and couldn't be helped anyway. The employees would sit in the break room and talk about the clients.

Telling what was said during their session and giving the clients' names; which was breaking confidentiality and very unethical. What disgusted me the most, is when I saw employees brushing their teeth in the break room sink. I felt like vomiting when I saw this." As Kris was explaining her dislike towards non-profit programs, Mr. Boss Man walks up to the desk of Anika and scolds her for talking while working. He embarrasses her in front of all the other employees to the point where she gets up and runs out of the building for a fifteen-minute break. She returns, quietly finishes her work, and with a feeling of shame and embarrassment rushes to her car and drives off. She's feeling so depressed now that she really does not have the enthusiasm within herself to go to classes. Before driving home, she goes to the university, walks over to her professor's office, and reads over her assigned work before turning it in.

CHAPTER 5 FOLLOWING YOUR HEART

Instead of going to classes Anika drives over to her boyfriend's house. He is asleep with the rays of sunlight hitting his face through the window. After the third knock he answers. The wrath of anger in his tone pierces her ears like a sonic boom.

"What in the hell are you doing here, you're supposed to be in class?" Mosi says.

"Oh, I thought you would be happy to see me, knowing that we don't get a chance to see each other that often," Anika says.

"I am happy to see you, but you are missing class. Do you do this all the time without me knowing? You've been acting weird for the past month. What's really going on? You never miss classes." Anika shifts her hips in a determined twist and shoves Mosi aside in order to enter his apartment.

"You know I can't believe you. I come all the way over here, and you are upset because I missed one class. You did not even ask me why. I had a bad day at work; I may even quit. Can I at least tell you about my—" He cuts her off.

"I don't care what happened at work; you got bills to pay. You act so retarded and careless sometimes. I am not paying for any of those bills that accrue while you decide to take a joy ride from your responsibilities. You're always quitting your jobs. You can't keep a job for nothing in the world. I think you've had about eleven jobs since I've known you," Mosi says.

"What do you mean? I don't live here with you, and the bills I pay are my business." Anika's voice augments at a higher pitch.

"You are wrong. It's our business. We are going to get married one day, and when we are married and if we ever want to buy a house, our credit must be tight. If not, we can't have anything. And I'm not about to allow you to mess that up for me," Mosi says as he paces the floor with a disturbed look on his face. Anika's temper inclined with forceful acceleration.

"Wait a minute, when did you ever propose to me for marriage? I'm confused. This argument is getting way out of hand. You are really out there," Anika says.

"Are you trying to call me crazy, because you know you are?" Mosi says.

"I am not, and I was not trying to call you crazy. What's wrong with you?" Anika's lungs burst into a flame of fury.

"Oh, I'll tell you what's wrong with me!" Mosi blares.

"You've been cheating on me, haven't you? Be honest. You don't call me as much as you use to. You're beginning to break promises when it comes to seeing me. What's his name?" Mosi demands in an uproar of anger. He twists the edge of her shirt into a spiral lock and pulls her forward. "What's his name?" He pulls her closer to him and screams, "WHAT'S HIS NAME?!" With a strong grip Anika grabs Mosi's hand and yanks away her shirt and runs for the door. He allows her to leave. He looks out of the window as she is running for her car.

He thinks to himself, I know she's cheating on me and I will get to the truth. I can't believe this is happening. God, I hope she's not. She better not be. We have been together for eight years. How can she ruin eight years? I know I've done things in my past. But I am over that now. I'm not that way anymore. But I know she is doing something. Even if she ain't cheating, she is doing something wrong. Can't believe she missed class. Those classes and her job use to be important to her. "WHAT'S GOT INTO HER?!" Mosi screams until the rippled sound of his voice reaches Anika's ears. As Anika is leaving, he notices she has dropped two of her unedited essays. He leaves his apartment, goes down stairs picks up her essays and begins to read.

For the first time, Mosi sees the true beauty in Anika. He never really realized the insight and wisdom that his love had possessed.

Anika is so upset as she is driving, she puts in one of her favorite songs. She sings as she cries in the hopes of feeling better. I want you to love me, to hold me, forever. I want you to love me, to hold me, forever…she thinks as she drives. He can't give me what I really want and desire, but I know who can. She calls upon the only one that can truly love her without judgment, blame, or shame. She then calls her new friend David.

"Hello," David says.

"Hey, how are you doing?" Anika says.

"I'm doing fine, but something is not right with you. What's wrong?" David says while giving her his sympathetic ear.

"Oh I'm OK, it's just… I'm having problems again in my relationship."

"Is he acting paranoid again," David says.

"Yes, he thinks I'm cheating, which I could if I wanted to, but I'm not," Anika says.

"Look, I know you feel uncomfortable about coming over here, but you're down, and I think I can cheer you up," David says.

"And how do you plan to cheer me up?" Anika asks as the right corner of her mouth stretched sideways in interrogation.

"I'm just your friend. You don't have to be afraid that I might get close to you unless you want me to," David says. She is briefly hesitant, but then decides to head toward his place. After the first knock he answers.

"Oh that was quick," Anika says.

"What was quick?" David asks.

"You answered the door really quick. I was expecting to wait."

"Oh no, it's getting late. I would never have you waiting outside for me at night," David says.

"Oh, you're so sweet," she says sarcastically.

"Please sit down and let me show you something," David says. She sits down and patiently waits until he comes out of the bedroom. She is almost afraid to find out what he is about to show her. Anika glances around his efficiency. The lights are dim. His tangerine lava lamps serve as a night light. His plaid futon leans up against his lime walls. His end tables where his lamps rest are made of cheap wood. Thrown up against his floor is a dingy rug and right above is a painting of an apricot tiger that startles Anika at first glance.

"Here, take a look at this" David says. "What's this?" Anika says.

"They're songs; I'm a songwriter," David says.

"Oh, you are. That would make sense, since you are so talented. Read some to me." He pulls out one of his songs and begins to sing. "I've been watching you from afar, and I would like to know what kind of women you are, look so good you really blowing my mind, I would like to know, can I give it to you."

"Oh, that sounds nice. I did not know you could sing," Anika says.

"Oh yes, I can. Listen to the second verse.

"The night is young and you're all alone, I need a woman I can call my own. Let me feel your…"
Her brows lift in intoxication.

"Oh, I've heard enough; you can be famous. You are so talented. Unbelievable. I can't believe I know—"
David cuts her off. His right hand motions a firm cessation.

"Please do not exaggerate," David says.

"I'm not; really that's good."

"Why do you always think I'm pulling your leg when it comes to how talented you are? I would not lie to you. You could really be a star one day," Anika says.

"You think so," David says. "Yes I do," Anika says.

"Thank you. I think I'm good at what I do. It's just that I am really careful about sharing my dreams with others. I've decided to keep dreams to myself until I start making money. If I meet someone who has achieved success that's in line with what I'm striving for, I'll considering sharing.

But I do appreciate your encouragement," David says. He then gets so excited he places his sweaty palm on her heart.

"Whenever he makes you cry, you think of me here. I love you." She lifts his hand from her bosom.

"Oh, you're talking crazy. You don't love me. It's too soon to love me. We've only known each other for a month."

"You can't put time on love. I knew I loved you when I first laid eyes on you. You do something to me that I can't explain," David says.

"Why are you telling me this? You know I have someone. And you promised that you would not try anything."

"Yes, I did. I said I wouldn't pursue you unless you wanted me to and I know you want me," David says.

"I don't want you. You're wrong." Her feet make a motion towards the door. A web of hard flesh tightly grabs her from behind. He presses his hungry lips on the base of her bare neck. She cannot deny the passion that he brings forth.

"Oh, you feel so good to me. Let me have you. Please." She lifts her arms to escape his web of desire. "NO."
He stops, looks at her without saying a word. And then he sits down right next to his music.

"I'm sorry. I should not have done that. I apologize," David says. Anika sees blood rush throughout David's face with humiliation. He steps away from her to demonstrate his willingness to honor her request.

"You're damn right," Anika says.

"Please sit down; let's just talk. Share with me some of your talents. What are your talents?"

With a look of caution she steps nearer to him while keeping sight of his tempting hands. She gracefully sits on his futon with her head down and says, "I have none."

"Oh, that can't be true. I don't believe that. What are your dreams? Everyone has a dream; something to live and love for," David says.

"I have no dreams," Anika says.

"Come on. Have you ever tried to write?" David asks.

"No. The only time I write is when I do those stupid essays for class," Anika says.

"Stupid, I bet they are good. Recite some to me," David says. "Do you really want to hear them?"

"Yes. To me you are a little bird. As soon as you find your true calling you're going to soar like a wild eagle. You're just a diamond in the rough right now, that's all," David says. Without hesitation she heads toward her car to retrieve her essays, and only finds two; the other two are missing. She runs back upstairs to his apartment.

"Oh, I can't believe I have lost two of my essays," Anika says.

"Don't worry, they will turn up." She hands her essays to him and he reads out loud.

"These essays are really good and I can clearly understand that your main points are to stand up for what you believe in and to believe in God," David says. Anika looks over her essays again. "Yeah, you're right; this is what I am trying to say."

"If I am correct in my interpretations of your essays, why is it that you say you have no dreams?" David asks.

"I just don't know what it is I want to do with my life. All I know is that I want to help other people, find true love, and find my true calling. Those are my goals," Anika says.

"Well, I believe you can have all of that." His firm arms embraces her body tightly. It feels so good she does not want him to let her go. David braces her by the wrist, walks her over to his stereo and plays his favorite song. To his surprise, she begins to sing to him. "The way I love him, I will never love another. The way I love him, no one else desires my lovin'. The way I love him, I will never love another. The way I love him, no one else desires my lovin'. No more lonely nights I have to suffer. No more tears have to fall. No more nights feeling like dying. No more years all alone." He begins to laugh.

"Why are you laughing?" Anika asks.

"You have talent but singing is not it, but I thank you for that song. We have the same passions," David says. He touches her heart again, braces her wrist once more, and they walk together towards his bed. They awaken together.

CHAPTER 6 LOSING HIM

The date is March 1, 2000. The time is 8:00 a.m. Anika realizes she is late for work; almost an hour late. As she is departing from David's home, her cellular phone rings. It's her boyfriend.

"Where have you been? I've been calling all night!" Anika lies for the first time.

"I was at my mom's house asleep. I'm sorry I did not hear my cell ring. I know my battery is low; my phone must have gotten shut off. I'm so sorry."

"All right," Mosi replies.

"Well, I'm already thirty minutes late for work so I'll call you later," Anika says.

"All right, bye," he says with a tone of anger.

She arrives to work forty-five minutes late and her supervisor immediately calls her into his office and slams the door. All employees including the therapist are watching the door wondering what is being said. "You have received a verbal and written warning about being late. You have received warnings about talking while at work. And this behavior continues. I have no choice but to let you go," Mr. Boss Man says. She begs and pleads for her job.

"Please don't fire me. I have responsibilities. I have an apartment. I have bills to pay. The only reason I have been coming in late is because I have been having trouble sleeping for the past few months," Anika says.

"No more excuses, please get your things," Mr. Boss Man says as he breaks eye contact, turns, and walks away. With tears racing from her soul, she pitter-patters sluggishly over to her desk and begins packing up her things.

"I'm so sorry, is there anything I can do?" Kris asks.

"No, there's nothing you can do. I'll call you." Anika rushes out of the office. She then drives over to her boyfriend's home. After the third knock he answers. Anika speaks first.

"Have you seen my two essays? I've been working on all four of my essays this past month and I must turn them in."

"What are you doing here? I thought you were supposed to be at work," Mosi says.

"Don't start with me today; I just got fired," Anika says.

"Fired! How can you get fired? You've been working there for a year. That does not sound right. You can never keep a job. Are you missing days at work like you're missing days in school? What's going on?" Mosi asks as his facial muscles tighten.

"There's nothing going on," Anika says. Mosi grabs her cellular phone and dials up the last unknown number called. David answers, "Hello."

"Who is this?" Mosi asks.

"Who is this?" David asks with a voice of confusion.

"Who is David?"

"How did you know his name?" Anika asked.

"It's right here on your phone. You thought you could hide this from me!" Mosi says.

In hearing the confusion, David hangs up. Mosi is so stricken with hurt, he needs not to ask any more questions. He knows the truth and storms into the bedroom and slams the door.
She does not fight. After an hour he comes walking out of the room with a towel and swimming trunks in his hand. He walks out of the apartment, slams the door, and decides to go downstairs to take a swim.

This is when it all began, when she began to lose everything. She runs after him with her cellular phone in her hand.

"Baby," Anika says. He turns, looks at her, and continues stumping towards the pool.

"He is just a friend," she screams out, "nothing happened, please believe me."

"No, you're nothing but a liar. How can I believe anything you say?" The phone rings, it's David again. Mosi tries to snatch the phone away from her. They both fight over the phone and both end up falling onto the pool deck. The struggle for the phone is so intense Mosi falls into the deep end of the water and hits his head on the bottom of the pool.

"Oh, God, oh, oh, my God!" She wants to swim over to the deep end to save him but she cannot swim. She instead gets out of the pool, runs over to the front office and gets the attention of one of the managers. The manager comes running out like a superman, jumps into the pool and saves her boyfriend. But Mosi had been in the pool for too long. He is now unresponsive and cannot move. The manager tries CPR and yells for Anika to call the ambulance.

Seven minutes later the ambulance arrives and drives Mosi to the hospital and she follows in her car.

"He is in a coma," the doctor says. He may not make it. Anika's heart races through her chest and her body falls limply onto the now beaten floor. She then calls upon her best friend. She gives Mary a call.

"Hey, Mary, how are you doing?" Anika asks.

"I'm fine and yourself," Mary replies.

"I'm not doing so well; did you hear?"

"Hear what?" Mary asks.

"My boyfriend fell into a coma," Anika says.

"Oh, my God. I'm so sorry to hear that. How did it happen?" Mary asks.

"Oh, it is too painful for me to talk about right now," Anika says.

"I understand; do you want to come by for a drink?" Mary asks.

"Sure," Anika replies. She then drives over to Mary's house. After the first knock, Mary answers.

"Hey, girl, you're doing all right?" asks Mary.

"I don't know. I feel so bad. I feel like I want to die. I don't know what I would do if I lost him. My whole life would be over," Anika says.

"That's not true; you have a lot to live for. I can't believe you are talking like that. Maybe you need to call your mom. On second thought, I'll call her for you." Mary picks up her phone and dials for Ms. Muhammad.

"Ms. Muhammad, I think you need to speak with your daughter, she doesn't sound too good," Mary says.

"What's wrong, Anika?" Ms. Muhammad asks.

"Mosi fell into a coma. And I feel so bad I don't know what to do," Anika says.

"How did it happen?" Ms. Muhammad asks.

"I'll tell you more about it later; it's just too painful to discuss right now. I am so hurt. I don't know what to do," Anika says.

"Don't worry. A coma is very unpredictable. A lot of people who fall into comas come out quickly. Talk to him, touch him and have faith that he will be among those who snap out of it. Reassure him that you love him unconditionally; he can hear you. Above all, be patient. Mosi will be fine and so will you. God doesn't put anything on you that you can't handle. We'll talk tonight. I love you," Ms. Muhammad says.

"You feel better, don't you? Your mom always cheers you up. I need your advice about this guy I met. He's incredibly overbearing at times; to the point where it makes me scared, but my feelings for him are growing stronger by the day. I'm so confused. What do you think?" Mary says.

"I'm pretty sure you will figure it out," Anika says with a fuming tone to her voice.

"No, I need your input, your advice," Mary says.

"I don't know what to tell you. I don't know him. I'd rather not judge him," Anika says.

"But he beats me; what should I do? Should I leave him?"

"You are smart enough to make your own decisions," Anika says. Mary begins to become frustrated.

"Last Tuesday he actually hit me in my—"

Anika cuts her off. "Look, I know what you're trying to do; you're trying to get me to make your decisions for you, but I can't. You know how I feel about abusive men, and you know what I would do about it so that should be enough. I think you love drama too much," Anika says.

"I do not," Mary says. Anika then changes the subject.

"I need a favor; I need to stay at your place for a week. I just feel too—"

Mary cuts her off. "It's OK; I understand, you can stay here as long as you like and you have perfect timing because I invited other friends to stay with me for the entire week also. We're going to have so much fun, believe me."
There's a knock at the door; it's Mary's friends.

"Oh, speak of the devil," Mary says. She opens the door.

"Hey what's up, Rachel and Tonya? Did you bring the stuff?" Mary says.

"Heck yeah, you know it," Rachel says. Mary grabs the sack of marijuana. "Who has a match?"

"Right here," Tonya says. "Light it up," Mary says.

Anika sits there quietly appalled by what she is seeing. Her friends are doing DRUGS in front of her.

"Oh, I'm being rude; let me introduce you. Tonya, this is my friend that I was telling you about; I've known her for six years." Tonya is an attractive young woman with a bright yellow complexion and long honey-blonde hair. Her turquoise blouse and tight-fitting capris matched her eyes.

"Do you smoke?" Tonya asks.

Mary replies, "Oh no, she does not smoke, she doesn't do anything. She doesn't even like taking aspirin; she's a virgin to everything." Tonya and Rachel throw back their heads forcing pressure against the air as they laugh, infectiously.

"That's not true," Anika says.

"Yes, it is true. You know you try to act like you perfect sometimes," Mary says.

"I am not perfect just because I don't smoke. And I know why you smoke, Mary," Anika says.

"Why do I smoke?" Mary says.

"You smoke to relieve some of your anxiety. I noticed every time you get depressed or anxious, you smoke. Every time you're confronted with a problem you can't solve, you smoke," Anika says.

"That's not true," Mary says.

"Yes it is," Anika begins to giggle.

"You don't need to smoke; all you have to do is get to the root of your problems. Developing healthy, productive habits like exercising, eating right and maybe even reading will lower your anxiety level. You don't want to be depressed all the time." Mary's eyes have a look of jealousy.

"There you go again, Thinking you know everything. And, oh yeah, did I tell you all, she's getting married."

"What, I never said I was getting married," Anika says. Tonya says,

"You're getting married? To who? What's his name?" Anika is quiet and says nothing. "How long y'all been together?" Tonya asks.

"For a while," Anika says.

"I wanna know how long," Tonya says.

"I'm not telling you how long because I don't like your tone of voice. All you are doing, for whatever reason, is trying to get into my business so you can dig up some dirt to create some drama and then gossip. I am not getting married," Anika says.

"Well, you did say you wanted to get married," Mary says.

"That's right. I said I wanted to get married. I did not say I was getting married," Anika says.

"The marriage won't work out anyway," Tonya says. Anika is silent for she knows if she allows silence, the truth of Tonya's thoughts will be spoken.

"I, I mean it may not work out. I was almost married and found out my fiancé was cheating," Tonya says.

"So you're trying to give me advice based on your own experience, which is what people usually do," Anika says.

"All men are dogs. Why you want to marry him, anyway? From what I hear, he ain't got no money, anyway. He's broke. What he gonna do for you? Love don't pay the bills. If a man ain't got no money, he don't get no loving from me. I might give him some on credit, but if I'm not paid back, he gets rejected. See yah," Tonya says.

"You sound like a gold digger," Anika says. Tonya then gets offended. "I am not a gold digger. I make sure my man is satisfied."

"What about love," Anika says.

"Love, love, take a love check down to your electric company and let's see how fast it bounces. A man hasta have money; good money, to mess with me. I'm no gold digger. I just know what it takes to make a relationship work. Money, money, money," Tonya says.

"Leave her alone, Tonya. She just may be happy. And besides, who told yah he ain't got no money? He's an electrical engineer. He got plenty money. And from what I hear, not only does he have money, he's good in bed." Rachel says.

"Oh, is that right?" Tonya says with a look of curiosity like she wants to know for herself how good in bed Mosi really can be. Anika then turns and firmly stares into Mary's eyes.

"What are you doing telling my business like that?" Anika says.

"Don't blame me; blame Rachel. She's the one with the big mouth," Mary says. Rachel sits there dumbfounded and does not say a word. Anika then glances at the television set. There is a documentary on of Hitler's life story. Everyone remains silent for five minutes listening to the tragedy of the holocaust. Anika looks over to Mary.

"You know I used to be Hitler in my past life," Anika says. Tonya, Mary, and Rachel pause and look at each other.

"I think this marijuana is getting to your friend," Tonya says. Anika sits up from the couch and walks towards the 19-inch black and white television and kneels on the bare cold floor.

She stares with a blank look at the television.

"Anika, are you OK? You're acting a little strange," Mary says.

"I killed all those people, but it happened in my former life. As soon as I killed myself my soul went right back in utero to become reborn. I now have a beautiful spirit. Can you forgive me?" Anika says. Nervously, knees shaking, Rachel stands up from the couch and takes two steps backwards.

"You're really scaring me, Anika. Maybe we should not smoke around you," Rachel says.

While continuing to stare at the television set, Anika sees a vision of Jesus. He appears to her in just as perfect form and image as the paintings on Mary's wall. She then hears Jesus speak, "I am the son of God." Then just as fast as he appears, he leaves her vision.

"Did you see him? Did you see Jesus?" Anika turns and looks at her friends. Words are stuck within their throats.

"Did you see him? Did you see Jesus?" Anika repeats once more.

"Anika, you're really scaring us. I thought you were Muslim?" Mary says.

Anika then stares back at the television set. An unseen man's voice begins to speak to only her. "I know it's hard for you to concentrate now, but I need for you to listen. This is very important. Abuse, mental illness, AIDS, vitamin C, flowers."

"Did you hear that? Did you hear a man's voice?" Anika says.

"No," Tonya says.

"Maybe you ought to lie down. I don't think you're feeling so good." Anika then goes into the bedroom and falls asleep.

When Anika awakens she decides to drive over to Bayfront Hospital to visit Mosi. When she walks in she notices two women standing beside Mosi's bed. One is an older woman who looks to be in her forties who weighs about 360 pounds; the other in her twenties. The older woman notices Anika first. She looks up with a venomous complex look on her face and says,

"How do you know my son?"

"I'm his girlfriend of eight years," Anika says.

"My son never spoke of you," Ms. Sultan says. There then is a silence for one minute. Anika is speechless. Anika then sits on the opposite side of the bed and holds Mosi's hand. Ms. Sultan never removes her eyes from Anika.

"How did this happen to my son? Someone must know something."

"He hit his head on the bottom of the pool," Anika says with shame.

"How can he injure himself in a pool? My son knows how to swim, he was in the boy scouts for four years," Ms. Sultan says.

"I'm sorry but that's how it happened," Anika says.

"Were you there when it happened?" Ms. Sultan asks.

"Yes I was," Anika says.

"And you couldn't save him from this, and you're supposed to be his girlfriend of eight years. Do you realize that he is in a coma? Do you know how serious this is?" Ms. Sultan says.

"It's not my fault," Anika says.

"Do you feel guilty, because I never said it was your fault? I think you know something. Something else happened to cause my son to hit the bottom of the pool deck. And when he awakens I will find out," Ms. Sultan says.

Anika is once again silent.

"Can I be with him in private? I come to save his life. All it takes is a touch from my hand and he will be well again," Anika says. Ms. Sultan gives Anika a weird look.

"Oh, no. Me and my daughter will be sitting right over here while you have your moment with him." Ms. Sultan and her daughter walk over to the other side of the room while keeping their eyes on Anika.

Anika whispers, "Baby, I'm so sorry this had to happen. I love you so much. I want you to pull out of this for me; you can do it. You're strong. Everything is going to be fine. I promise you."

Ms. Sultan walks over to Anika. "Why are you talking to him? He can't hear you; He's in a damn coma," Ms. Sultan says. Anika then kisses him on his forehead and then exits the room without saying a word to Mosi's relatives. She then gets into her car to drive back to Mary's house. She puts in one of her favorite CD's, plays number 9, and begins to sing while crying, "I'm missing you. I was once a part of you, now I'm here feeling all alone, feel a need to sing this song. I'm missing you. I'm missing what we used to share. How you were always there. I'm missing you. I'm missing the love you used to give. The love you used to share. One day I'll come back to you. Come home to see you. I'm missing you."

Anika then pulls up to Mary's house and everyone's sitting outside the apartment.

"Where have you been? We were all worried. You just left out of here without saying a word." Mary says.

"I'm sorry. I had to go and see Mosi," Anika says.

"How is he doing?" Rachel says.

"He's still in a coma," Anika then begins to cry.

"His mother was so mean to me. She didn't even know who I was. Mosi never told her about me," Anika says.

"All these years and his mother don't know about you. That's kind of strange. Don't you think?" Rachel says.

"I don't think it's weird. Some men don't introduce their girlfriends until they're ready for marriage," Mary says.

"Well, after eight years you should be ready for marriage," Rachel says. Mary gives Rachel a disapproving look and then walks over to comfort Anika.

"Everything is going to be fine," Mary says. Anika then walks over to the door, stands on a chair, and begins nailing three bolt locks. Rachel, Tonya, and Mary look up at her.

"What are you doing?" Mary asks.

"They're coming to get me. The government can see through these walls. They know every move I make. They have been tapping my phone calls. I hear a clicking sound every time I'm on the phone. I have to make sure they do not get in," Anika says, eyes wide.

"She's acting weird again," Rachel says.

"I think she's joking. Anika, come down from there. Go and get some more rest. I think you're paranoid from the marijuana," Mary says. Anika does as requested. They all continue smoking each day for seven days. On Sunday, Anika just cannot take any more of the marijuana and decides to leave. Anika goes home high as a kite. Before opening her door she notices a letter shoved underneath her door. She pulls the letter out and reads:

This is an eviction notice. You have three days to pay in full $360. If this amount shown is not paid within three days, the eviction process will begin.

She then calls up David.

"David, I need your help."

"How could you call me? I have not spoken to you for more than a week. What's going on?" David says.

"Everything is going wrong. I just found out that I'm going to be evicted and also my boyfriend found out about us and he's now in a coma," Anika says.

"What happened?" David asks.

"It's too painful for me to talk about right now, I'm so upset," Anika says.

"Does it have anything to do with me?" David asks.

"Yes. He called your number," Anika says.

"Oh, that was him on the other end of the phone the other day?" David says.

"Yes," Anika says.

"What did he do? He didn't hurt you, did he?" David asks. "No," Anika says.

"Because of what happened, I'm feeling guilty now," David says.

"No. It's not your fault, it's mine," Anika says.

"Will he be OK?" David asks.

"I don't know," Anika says.

"I can't believe I'm feeling sorry for the man that's in love with the same women I'm in love with," David says.

"You're in love with me?" Anika asks.

"Of course; you know I am. I love everything about you," David says.

"What about—"

"I know what you're about to say. My color and your color mean nothing to me. I love you regardless and I don't care who knows," David says.

"I wasn't speaking about our different races; you know that I am not prejudiced. I was speaking about Mosi. I love him and I will never leave him for anyone."

"Please don't say that. If you only knew how much I love you, you would not say that," David says. She then becomes nervous.

"I'm sorry. It's the truth. Listen I feel really anxious right now and I'm having a hard time calming myself down." David remains silent.

"Well, what should I do?" Anika says.

"What do you usually do to calm yourself down?" David asks.

"Usually I exercise or read a book when I become anxious, but I don't feel like doing either of them," Anika says.

"What do you do when you're feeling anxious?" Anika asks.

"I write music; you should do the same," David says.

"Do what?" Anika says. "Write," David says.

"But I am not a talented writer," Anika says.

"That's not true; you can write. Write some of your essays for me. Writing will calm you down," David says.

"OK. I'll try and then I'll call you later,"

She thought of the love she had for both Mosi and David and she wrote.

After writing she gives David a call.

"You were right; writing does help calm me. But I'm still worried about my rent. Do you have $360 that I can borrow?" Anika asks.

"I think I may be able to scrape up that amount. When do you need it by?" David asks.

"I need it now," Anika replies.

"Don't worry, beautiful, I will take care of it," David says.

CHAPTER 7 MENTALLY ILL

Anika is at Mosi's apartment. It is now 3:30 a.m. Torrential thunder and rain is pouring down as she decides to clean. She does what she must always do before cleaning; she puts in music. She begins to play one of her favorite songs, "All Eyes on Me" by one of her favorite artists. As she listens to the words they began to speak to her.

She turns off the music and sits in absolute silence. The song begins playing in her head, without the CD. Something is terribly wrong, yet Anika is unaware. She suddenly has an idea, her eyes widening like a deer in headlights. She did as one of her professors taught and searched the Internet for anything having to do with Tupac. She found that there was a professor in another state who taught a class on his poetry. She was so excited and begin printing off this material so she could show her friends. Something then happened; something she could not explain.

She could no longer communicate sensibly. She was aware of her surroundings, of what she was doing and unable to control her actions. She became temporarily insane. As she stares out of the window, she first begins to see colors; varying hues of purple.

"Oh, this is so beautiful." She then knocks her hand up against the window hitting it three times. She begins to ramble, "Bermuda triangle, pyramids, one two three corners means you. If we build the pyramids, they will show themselves. But we must be accurate. As the Egyptians surely were, they built it and they came."

She then points her finger straight out into the air and pretends to connect the dots of a pyramid, then points her finger through the imaginary triangle that she has created. While looking out of the window she makes both the thumbs-up and peace sign. "I am you and you are me and we are we," Anika rambles. She looks up to the east and sees in the clouds an outline of a man's face. She then quickly looks away and began to feel as if someone was controlling her thoughts. "Do you know who you are? You're the one." She opens the curtains wider and begins pointing at people and cars passing by outside.

"The matrix is coming. Revolution. We can all save this planet together." She then runs into the bedroom, snatches the bedspread off the bed, places it around her body, and says, "I'm a virgin. I must cover up. We all started off pure until someone abused us turning us into criminals. We're all virgins. The world is going to end, but I can stop it." She runs back into the living room. "Let's all hold hands. Give me your hand. We don't have to die." She then grabs the hand of what to her appears to be a ghost wrapped in a white hospital robe.

"Help me I need your help," she yells. "Those kids." She begins to cry. "All of the kids. Help them; they are scared. They need your help. 911. 211. September the eleventh. What happened on September the eleventh? All those people! The smoke kept rising and rising and rising.

The cowboy Bill is a part of this. He can stop this. He has a back problem. He can stop this before June 6 of 2006," Anika rambles. The rambling continues and wouldn't make sense to anyone, but Anika or someone who was trained in the field of mental health. The shadows from her lamps appear to her as UFOs. "If you build the pyramids, they will show themselves. If you stare hard enough into the field, you will see their map. The map to their universe." She then begins to scream, "Leave them alone; they're of peace!" She begins to sing, "The world needs our love. The world needs our love. We're deprived of love, so the world needs our love."

Anika then begins to whisper, "This is real. Believe me, my faith is strong. We are alive. We are all truly alive. Stop trying to explain it. Believe in the unseen. Believe in yourself. Forgive him for you are Him and He is you. You are she and she is you. You're not going to hell. You're already in a physical hell. Don't put yourself in a spiritual hell. Go to Him when you pass. Do not enter the left door, that's the dark side. You must enter the right door. Go to God, He loves you."

"There is a God! There is a God!" she begins to shout. "God won't let this happen! Charts can be reversed. I can save the world!" Anika screams. She lies on the floor with her arms crossed as if she is in a coffin. She then feels as if she is slowly dying. She puts things in threes. Things began to make sense to her. She begins to speak underneath her breath. "Three best friends, three movies, three influential professors that worked for the President, three relatives I get along with most, three song writers I love most, three directors, three articles of clothes, three shoes, three purple dresses, three enemies, three classes, three true loves, three…"

She feels as if she is losing her mind. Saying things in threes somehow comforts her making her feel like her mind at least has some sort of organization. She then tries to dial 911, but accidentally dials 211.

"Good evening how may I help you?" the counselor asks.

"I feel as if I'm going crazy. I need some help!" Anika screams. The counselor politely asks Anika to describe all of her symptoms. "I'm having racing thoughts, a hard time concentrating, I'm hallucinating, I've torn up my room, I'm putting things in threes, I can't breathe, I'm shaking, I'm crying constantly, I'm losing track of time, I'm paranoid."

Once the counselor analyzes the situation, he comes to the conclusion that she needs stabilization and refers her to the nearest crisis unit for the "mentally insane." Anika then hangs up the phone, grabs her car keys, and immediately runs down the stairs to her car. On the way to the crisis unit she continues to see colors.

Then she begins to speak. "I'm crying." She pauses and says, "I'm dying." She pauses and says, "No, I'm not dying. My big day is my wedding day. I'm flying. On that day, everyone will surround me with hugs and kisses and I will be truly happy for the first time. I'm not dying. I'm really flying." She begins to sing, "I think I'm flying way up high. I think I'm flying way up high. I'm in the sky, flying. I'm going to be ok."

She closes her eyes and begins to feel as if she is on an airplane for the first time. She truly thinks that she is flying and it's a very disturbing feeling for her. Her breath is taken away from her.

Anxiety paralyzes each of her muscles. She begins to sing again, "If you believe you will fly, above the highest sky. You will fly, above the highest clouds. You will fly if you believe you can fly. You will fly above the highest sky. You will fly above the highest clouds. You will fly. If you believe you can fly."

She then becomes observant, noticing very specific characteristics about the cars in the area; from their rear view mirrors, to their colors, hues, and shapes. She believes she sees thirty-foot poles connect to the base of dome-shaped buildings, a face without a body that is smaller than the sun. In her mind, it has a transparent energy void of color with a stern look on his face and mouth slightly ajar. Anika then looks away and continues driving. The towering sun disappears before her eyes. The sky lightens a rosy violet, pastel color. Streaks of what appear to her as purple lighting, pelts against the sky. Moonstone towers in Greco-Roman style appear in front of her car. She places the back of her left hand across her eyes, fearing she will collide. Apprehension rushes from her throat.

She removes the back of her hand and sees a six--foot dragon fluttering belligerently toward her. His claws grip her windshield wipers. As she looked away he disappeared from her sight.

She made it to the hospital just in time as the staff immediately recognizes her symptoms as being out of the ordinary and possibly in need of care. They continue to observe her behavior as she begins to walk around the hospital holding the hands of passersby declaring her love for them and reassuring them that they are not ill.

She begins to point out the different colors in the room and says, "Red means stop; that lady is wearing red and white; don't bother her. Purple is of God; that lady is wearing purple; she's okay. Blue is a calm color, blue is okay." Three doctors approach her attempting to give her pills to calm her, but she refuses as she remembers the story told by the therapist about the children refusing to take medications for psychotic episodes.

The three doctors then locked her into a room surrounded by white walls, a video camera, and a white bed with side rails that, to her, resembled an angel's wings. Being locked into this room upset her and so she began to scream. "My soul is dying!" She begins to sing. She then shows her stomach, looks into the camera and says, "I'm a virgin. I've never had an abortion."

In her mind she thinks the hospital staff is talking about her. She pauses and says, "I only went to the abortion clinic because it was across the street from my job." She pauses and says, "Don't judge me. I try my best not to judge you." She then thinks of Hitler and begins saluting towards the camera.

She turns, hits her feet three times on the floor, walks backwards and then salutes to the camera. She then says, "Love me. I have the mark of the beast." She combs back her hair with her fingers and shows the camera a birthmark on the right side of her skull. She is quiet and then begins to speak. "We all have made mistakes in our lives. Get over it and grow. There's no reason to be living in misery and grief for years." She uses pantomime and sign language to communicate with others. She gives the finger and then speaks again.

The delusions and hallucinations continue and increase in their levels of incomprehensibility.

"We can all have peace, if you were not so afraid of your past mistakes and love yourself and the unseen." Matter-of--factly she states, "We must all learn sign language so those who are here can communicate with those who are home."

Anika continues to use hand gestures that make sense to her believing she is communicating effectively with the world around her. She speaks again, "Clearly, open your eyes, shut your mouth, and listen to what is being said. Be observant instead of nosy, be loving and sharing instead of pushy and con-trolling, truly love God and you can love yourself and others. You can have confidence. You can have anything and meet anyone you want if you shut your mouth and listen!"

She then thinks, no one will ever have to go through what I went through again! Believing she is screaming the sound of doves calling she screeches and is met with a syringe filled with Haldol, an antipsychotic, piercing her skin. Because of this injection she sleeps a full eight hours for the first time in two and a half days.

CHAPTER 8 MUSIC THERAPY

She awakens the next evening in a crisis unit for the mentally insane. It is now 4:45 a.m. and the unit is freezing cold and smells of dried blood. The unit is set up like a jail cell. All clients must eat, sleep, and take all breaks together. She can only watch TV, eat, take breaks and bathe when the unit's staff wants her to. The only privilege she has is to play her own music. The first person she sees is one of her best friends, the therapist, Kris. Kris cannot believe what she is seeing and immediately calls Anika's mother. "Ms. Muhammad, your daughter is very ill and is here in the facility where I work; come quickly," Kris says. Ms. Muhammad drops the phone, grabs some of Anika's things, and without haste drives to the crisis unit. Her daughter is so far gone in delirium and hallucinations, she does not even notice her own friend at first.

She gets up off the couch and goes into her room. Her mother arrives shortly thereafter, and is asked to wait until visiting hours begin before seeing her daughter. Ms. Muhammad then drops off three tapes that Anika loves and some articles of clothing.

Anika finally awakens and Kris gives her the music. She begins to play one of her favorite songs causing her to cry. She then says, "You can have anything you dream of if you just believe in your dreams. You are not dreaming." Then she hears a voice on one of her tapes.

It's the voice of Mary who is crying. Did Mary die? God, I hope not. Did I die or am I dying? She feels as if she is dying and holds out her arms for those loved ones to hug her and surround her with kisses, but they never do. She thinks, God, I hope I'm not dying. I have a lot more to accomplish before I pass. Did we all die? Then she says out loud, "My will is now strong. I am now of complete confidence. I know what my path is now and I must fulfill it. I'm the only one who has the right combination."

She begins to cry as she sings, "I will walk the dark for you, but only you. I would die for you, but only you. I will cry for you, but only you. Fire, hell, and rain won't keep me away." She then drops to her knees and screams out her love's true name. She speaks. "I know now whom I love the most." She begins to sing once more, "You are one in a million. You will love me always. You are one in a million, because you will love me always."

She breaks for silence and resumes speaking in a manner not easily understood by most, but certainly by Anika.

"No one ever has to go through what I went through again. I have the secrets. I have the secrets to happiness and to health. You can have a mental illness and not go crazy so shut up and listen. You're too busy talking to listen. I'm trying to show you. Open your eyes. Open your mind got dammit. We don't all have to die!"

She begins to think, "Was I put to the test? Am I being tested now? She then begins to sing, "I ain't scared to face the darkness. I'll never be scared." Anika begins to have flashbacks which create disturbing thoughts causing her to wonder about her life. "Is this the pain that is described as the pain of judgment day? Am I being judged right now? It is so painful but so beautiful!"

She screams, "God, am I dying?! No, I'm crying, no, I'm flying. Believe in me for I believe in myself and you. I have a right to dream let me fulfill my dreams. Wake up, wake up, wake up." She then sees a ghostly image of a woman dressed in a white dress that is burned at the bottom, sitting on the edge of her bed. She becomes so paranoid that she does not want to see that image again. Again she feels as if someone is controlling her thoughts. "You are the one. The one is whoever asks all the questions." Her two roommates look up at her in fear.

"Who is the one?" Ankia questions. "The one is the one who ask all the questions." This frightened Anika because she does not understand what the one means. She then begins to dance to another of her favorite songs. And her dance to others again makes no sense but to her it did. "I hear you, I see you, I feel you, and you are the light. You can see all. You are my eyes, my ears and my heart and I will walk for you. I need your help. I need your help. I need your help. I can't rest, I must rest, I need your help to rest." Anika's ramblings aren't making any sense, but to her the message is quite clear.

"I have waited an eternity for this; the time is now. I need for you to allow me to see through you, hear through you and feel the love of self and others through you. I need your help, I have waited an eternity and I must rest. I must meet him at 3:00 a.m. I will stay awake for an eternity to see his smile again to feel his touch again. I need to rest. I need to rest."

As she says those words she sees her friend the therapist and two doctors. They then gave her medication and she falls asleep. The next day she begins to see things a little clearer. She sees the therapist.

"How are you doing, are you OK?" the therapist asks.

Anika replies, "I'm back, I'm back. I'm OK as long as I rest. I need to rest. I need to go outside, the only time I feel peace is when all clients are outside taking their cigarette breaks."

Although Anika does not smoke she enjoys the breath of fresh air and her music that is played by the staff only during that time. The therapist then calls for an unexpected break, but this time the clients are not allowed to smoke. Anika and the other clients wake up from their zombie-like state. Every time the therapist asks a client to play a song that moves them spiritually, that client awakens. She notices that the songs that had themes about fulfilling dreams and having a love for God are the songs that seemed to wake the clients. When everyone wakes, Anika feels at peace.

"Oh, thank you," Anika thought. She looked up at the therapist once more. "Thank you, lady with wings."

The therapist looked down at her and says, "What do you mean?" She says very clearly, "Lady with dark purple wings. Thank you. Thank you for making the transition from home to here a whole lot easier. Now I can travel back and forth to many different homes as much as I want. Home is where the heart is."

"Who is the lady with wings?" the therapist asks.

"Thank you," Anika says. "If you can shut up and listen, I can bring you to your home, and show you you're not alone." She then grabs the therapist's hand. "Help me." She then screams, "Follow me! We can all have heaven here on earth if—" The therapist begins to feel scared and interrupts her. "If what, if what?" the therapist asks.

"Government," Anika mumbles.

"What?" the therapist asks.

"The government," Anika says.

"What about the government?" the therapist asks.

"Let me guide you; I will show you, shut your mouth," Anika says at a whisper. She then says, "Everyone needs to learn sign language, let me guide you. I have something very important to tell you, please listen." She remains silent for thirty seconds breathing heavily and resumes speaking. "It is 16th century BC. I'm not hallucinating. I'm not delusional. I'm not paranoid. There is no such thing as schizophrenia." She then is silent. "I can shut my mouth now."

She then wakes up completely and begins to clearly see her friend the therapist, begins to cry and thinks none of it was real. She then walks slowly with her head down, gazing at the floor painted with purple crosses, and heads back to her room shutting the door.

The therapist is baffled and is in shock that this is happening to Anika. When Anika enters her room, she sees one of her roommates hitting her head up against the wall. She walks over to her and sits next to her on her bed which is nothing more than a hard mat with cotton sheets draped across.

"Why are you hitting your head up against the wall?" Anika asks.

"I have no one. My mother left me when I was only six, and my father put me up for adoption. Now I have to deal with my annoying foster parents. They won't bring me any clothes. I ask for clothes and magazines and they won't bring them to me. I have to sit up in this jail cell wearing this stupid gown all day and I'm bored. There's nothing to do," Sharon says.

"I do know what you mean. Why are you here? What happened?" Anika asks yet another client. Engaging the other client in conversation seemed to create a sense of normalcy for Anika and brings at least some type of comfort to her new acquaintance.

"I couldn't sleep so I took a bunch of sleeping pills. My parents thought I was trying to kill myself and brought me here." The other roommate then interrupts.

"I slit my wrist. I can't even remember doing it. All I can remember is that I was at a party drinking, upset that my boyfriend was leaving town and I woke up here," Tammy says. Sharon then begins slamming her head against the wall until it bleeds.

"You're doing that for attention. You're not crazy. Why are you acting like you're crazy?" Anika asks.

"Everyone treats me like I'm crazy so I act crazy. You're the first person that's told me I'm not crazy," Sharon says.

"What do you mean she's not crazy? She's knocking her head up against the wall, for God's sake," Tammy says.

CHAPTER 9 EXPLANATION

In the morning, 7:00 a.m., a psychiatrist, a nurse, and a social worker awaken Anika.

"Follow me," the psychiatrist says. All four of them meet in what the clients refer to as the back room.

"You were unable to communicate sensibly for the past few days, what tragic event caused you to become unstable?" the nurse asks.

"I was hoping that you three would be able to tell me why I was in the condition that I was in." All three professionals are quiet and then the psychiatrist speaks.

"Were you around any marijuana or any substance that would impair your sleep?" Immediately she denies being around the drug, but then remembers that her friends were smoking marijuana around her for seven days and she did not want to get her friends in trouble.

"No. I have not been around any marijuana." All three professionals are silent once more. Then the nurse speaks, "After she is released she will be under the care of her mother." Then the nurse looks at Anika. The healthcare professionals were matter---of---fact and not at all caring in nature. "You will be released today." Then the nurse and psychiatrist leave her alone with the social worker. The social worker speaks for the first time.

"How is your relationship with your boyfriend?"

"My relationship is fine." She says nothing else and remains quiet for she knows the social worker is only trying to pry into her business and she will not let that happen. She will tell no one of her personal business. After five seconds she speaks again.

"I was around someone in a club who smokes marijuana, do you think that could have affected me? Because I don't do marijuana myself. Or do you think something is wrong with me? Do you think that I have a mental disorder?" Anika asks.

"Yes, it's a possibility that you may have schizophrenia, the results from the CAT scan show that your right temporal lobe is larger than most which is a sign of schizophrenia," the social worker says.

"But how could that be? I keep myself up, I'm not depressed, I don't attack people, I don't have a split personality, and I would never hurt myself, how could I have schizophrenia?" Anika says. Anika begins to breathe rapid breaths and begins to shake. "You're having a panic attack. Take a deep breath. I'm going to call Tom in to give you a shot," the social worker says.

"No, no shots. I'm not schizophrenic. I'm normal," Anika says.

"Yes you are normal. You're stereotyping the disorder which is what a lot of people do. Sixty-one percent of America thinks that people who are diagnosed with schizophrenia are violent. This is not true. Those with this disorder are rarely violent unless there's alcohol or drugs involved. And schizophrenics do not have a split personality. There's medication that can be prescribed and you can then be yourself—"

"No you're wrong. I don't have to take crazy pills."

"You were hallucinating and hearing voices," the social worker says.

"I was not hearing voices," Anika says.

"Yes, you were," the social worker says.

"No, I was not," Anika then says in an angry tone.

"You said while you were sick you heard the voice of Mary and you saw things that were not there," the social worker says.

"Those things I saw were there. There's nothing wrong with me. Just because you are not spiritual enough to see those things, you think I am crazy. Maybe there is something wrong with you. I know I am not crazy. I was not hallucinating. I saw a ghost, a ghost of a women that died by fire. She sat up from the edge of my bed and then walked out of my room," Anika says.

"That is not possible. There is no such thing as ghost. You were hallucinating," the social worker says.

"Isn't it a fact that in 1940 this building was actually a mansion owned by a rich woman who set her house on fire killing herself and her husband," Anika says.

"How do you know that?" the social worker says.

"I saw her. I saw that woman. She is still a ghost. She is not a spirit; she is a ghost," Anika says.

"This is ridiculous; you will be prescribed medication for your hallucinations and you must take this medication daily," the social worker says.

"I will not, there is nothing wrong with me," Anika says.

"Listen, there is nothing wrong with having to take medications," the social worker says.

"You are not listening to me, if you would just listen you would realize that I'm trying to tell you that I have been blessed to see these things. There is nothing wrong with me," Anika says. The social worker begins to listen at that point.

"You were seeing colors when you were sick; explain to me what it means to see colors," the social worker says.

"I saw shades of purple. Purple is a very spiritual color. I was touched by God. Before seeing what you call hallucinations, I did not have a full belief in God. Now I do," Anika says.

"You were hearing your friend Mary speak. But Mary was nowhere around. That means that you were hearing voices," the social worker says.

"No, I heard Mary crying on one of my tapes," Anika says.

"This is enough; you must take one tablet of Abilify daily. Twenty five milligrams, end of discussion. If you do not, chances are you will have another relapse or become suicidal." The social worker went on to explain mental health statistics as it relates to schizophrenia. "Ninety percent of persons who commit suicide have a mental or substance abuse disorder. Suicide is the eighth leading cause of death in the United States, claiming about 30,000 lives per year. So you must take your medication. You will be discharged in a few minutes and will be free to leave. You smoke marijuana don't you?" The social worker said.

Anika is quiet and says nothing knowing the silence will force the social worker to say what's really on his mind.

"I smoke marijuana," the social worker said. He then stood up wondering how Anika got him to confess his addiction. He was baffled. The social worker leaves the room and joins the psychiatrist and nurse.

"So what do you think?" the social worker says.

"I agree with the original diagnosis; she has paranoid schizophrenia," the nurse says.

"Yeah, I think you're right; she did say that she saw a ghost," the social worker says.

"A ghost. She saw a ghost?" the psychiatrist says.

"Yes she was also hearing voices and seeing different shades of purple and she wanted me to believe that this was all a spiritual occurrence. I don't understand what's so spiritual about seeing ghost, hearing voices, and seeing colors," the social worker says.

"Oh, there's nothing spiritual about seeing spirits; it's just downright crazy," the nurse says. The social worker and the nurse begin to laugh. The psychiatrist interrupts.

"I really don't think this is funny, I mean look at her, we usually don't get people in here like her. She's beautiful, she keeps up her appearance. Look at her skin, her teeth, her hair. I think this is a special case. I don't think we should laugh just yet. I think we should maybe listen to what she has to say," the psychiatrist says.

"Are you serious? Are you actually believing this stuff? Come on, you can't be serious," the social worker says.

"Oh, yes, I'm dead serious and let's be honest here, it's no secret that you, Alex, once saw a ghost," the psychiatrist says.

"I saw the holy spirit. That's what I saw," the social worker says.

"No. You saw a ghost or a spirit; not the holy spirit," the psychiatrist says.

The nurse then interrupts. "I can't believe we are here discussing spirits and ghosts. What's the difference anyway?"

"A spirit is of perfect form and a ghost, well, if you ever saw one you would know the difference," the psychiatrist says.

"Are you trying to say that you saw a ghost?"

"To be honest with you, yes. I did a little marijuana in my days and it caused me to hallucinate, so whether ghost are real or illusions I really could not tell you," the psychiatrist says.

"You did marijuana!" the social worker says.

"Oh, don't be so shocked. It's no secret that you are a marijuana junky. You're always so paranoid and jumpy all day long," the psychiatrist says. The nurse begins to laugh.

"Yeah he's right. You might have schizophrenia yourself."

"I'll tell you this, schizophrenia is the most difficult to diagnosis there is, and no one clearly knows what causes it nor how to permanently treat it. So you tell me, do some schizophrenics really see ghosts and spirits?" the psychiatrist says. This experience has moved Anika two steps closer to her true love. She receives a call while waiting in the crisis unit to be discharged.

Mosi has awakened from his coma.

"Unbelievable," Anika thinks.

"Oh, how are you doing?" Anika's parched lips stretched into a bright smile.

"I am doing better than I expected. The doctors are baffled from my quick recovery and so am I. I have so much to share with you but first I want to ask, will you marry me?" Mosi says. Shock rushes her eyes and racing heart. Her lashes swing in an upward motion.

"Yes I will. And I'm coming right over to see you." After being discharged from the crisis unit moments later, she runs to her car. She is so content now. Before driving off she puts in again one of her favorite CDs, song number 5, and she begins to sing, "I can feel you. My soul and heart feels you. I can see through you. I can feel through you. My soul and heart feels you."

Before she knows it with a blink of an eye she is at the hospital. She runs over to his room. She sees him, hugs him, and begins to shed perpetual tears of joy. "I love you so much."

"I love you, too," Mosi says. She takes his hand, walks him over to the window, stares out of the window, and listens to the beautiful sounds of birds chirping and says quietly, "Oh, God is good, this is true music."

She looks over to him and says, "I have a confession to make." She begins to cry once more. "I never cheated on you. I would never do that and I'm being honest. Although I did fall in love with another—"

He cuts her off. "I can't hear anymore."

"I know it's hard for you but I have to get this off my chest. I did fall in love with him. But it's over now and I promise you I will let him know that it's over. I just need to speak with him one more time."

"NO," Mosi says. "Just don't call him."

"Please listen. You don't understand. I can't just cut him off in that way. He's a nice guy, and he did nothing wrong. I'm the one who made the mistake. I need to be the one to break it off in the gentlest way possible. Please, you must understand. He has opened my heart to what love truly means. He has helped me bring out certain talents that I did not know I possessed." Mosi becomes furious.

"What? Are you saying that I could not do the same for you?"

"No. That's not what I'm saying. I'm just saying that he did this for me. And I truly believe that you, in time, could have done the same thing for me. It's just that I feel there's a lot of things within yourself that needs to be worked on before you can help me work on—"

He cuts her off once more. "I'm fine, In fact, I'm perfect. I do not need to work on anything. You need to work on yourself."

"I know I need to work on myself; this is what I was trying to say before you cut me off. And you are always cutting me off and you never listen. This is why you are so paranoid. You don't listen. You must listen to my entire thought process and then when I'm done you can speak. That way you will truly understand what I'm trying to say to you. And neither you nor I are perfect. No one's perfect. There's so much that I would love to share with you but I can only do so when you are ready to hear me. Please listen to me this time. I love you and I made a mistake, but I'm ready to move on if you are."

He looks down and says, "Yes I am." He looks up and stares into her eyes, holds onto the edge of her palm, and says, "I love you."

"I have something else to tell you. While you were in the hospital I became ill also," Anika says.

"No," Mosi replies hoping that it wasn't so.

"Yes I did. I just could not handle you falling into a coma. I felt it was my fault. I felt this would have never happened if I hadn't been seeing another man. I had to be baker acted," Anika says.

"I can't hear any more," Mosi says. Mosi wants to shut himself out of their agonizing conversation.

"Please listen. I was sent to a crisis unit; the same unit where my friend Kris works," Anika says.

"Oh God, she knows?" Mosi says.

"It's OK. She helped me out a great deal," Anika says.

"Did you go crazy?" Mosi asks.

"NO," Anika replies. You know I do not believe in that word. I don't know why I ended up in a crisis unit." He then shows a sign of weakness as a tear separates from his drowning pupils.

"Did you try to commit suicide?" Mosi asks.

"NO," Anika says.

"What happened right before you got ill?" Mosi asks.

"I stayed at Mary's house for a week," Anika says.

"Did she say or do anything that would have caused you to temporarily lose your mind?" Mosi asks.

"I don't know. What kind of question is that? I think the marijuana may have played a part," Anika says.

"Marijuana! They were doing drugs? How could you stay there if they were doing drugs?" Mosi asks. Anika hears panic in Mosi's voice.

"I did not think the drugs would affect me and I still don't know if they did. I thought as long as I did not smoke I would be OK," Anika says.

"Yes, but do you know that there is such thing as being a passive smoker?" Mosi asks.

"Yeah, you're right, but that could not have been the only factor. I saw things when I got sick," Anika says afraid of Mosi's reaction.

"What do you mean you saw things?" Mosi asks.

"I saw a ghost. I saw a man's face in the clouds. I saw futuristic buildings. And I saw colors." Anika says.

"That's too creepy for me, please," Mosi says.

"But I have to tell you. It was very creepy for me also. Even though I could not control what I was doing, I was still able to remember everything that happened to me, like I was in a trance of some sort. I remember very vividly seeing the ghost. Whether or not it was a hallucination, I do not know. The things I saw were so frightening for me I had to turn away quickly each time I saw it," Anika says.

"How did the ghost look?" Mosi asks.

"It appeared to be a Caucasian woman in a beautiful white dress that was burned at the end."

"Oh, that's creepy," Mosi says as his head and shoulders jerk backwards with a motion of revulsion.

"I know," Anika says.

"Did you see her face?" Mosi asks.

"No, I only saw her from the back," Anika says.

"Then how do you know it was a woman?" Mosi asks.

"By the fact that she had on a dress," Anika says. "Oh, it was so scary."

"How long did you see her for?" Mosi asks.

"Only for a few seconds, then I turned away quickly. I saw her as she walked from one room to another," Anika says.

"Oh, that is so scary. Did the doctors prescribe anything for your hallucinations?" Mosi asked.

"Yes, they prescribed Abilify, but I am not gonna take it anymore because I don't believe I was hallucinating. Those things I saw really did exist in another realm," Anika says. Mosi begins to jounce back and forth, eager to hear more.

"What else did you see?" Mosi asks.

"I saw the color purple," Anika whispers.

"What do you mean?" Mosi asks.

"Just as I said, I saw different shades of purple," Anika says. "Well, did you have your glasses on?" Mosi asks.

"NO," Anika says.

"Well, that could have been the result of blurred vision," Mosi says.

"Yes, this is possible. But why do you think I was focusing so much on the purple?" Anika asks.

"I don't know," Mosi says with curiosity. "What else did you see?"

"I can't tell you everything," Anika says.

"Why?" Mosi asks.

"Some things might be too much to hear," Anika says.

"Try me," Mosi says.

"Maybe another time," Anika says. He then becomes extremely anxious and says, "Let's set a date now for our wedding."

Mosi's fingers slip sensuously in between hers and he walks her over to the wall calendar in his hospital room.

"Let's set our wedding date a little over one year from now on June 6, 2001. How does that sound?"
She jokes around with him.

"I'm thinking more on the lines of six years from now; let's set the date for June 6, 2006."

"Oh, I don't think I can wait that long," Mosi says.

"Oh, I'm just joking. One year from now sounds fine. Let's get you out of here. Did the doctors say it's OK to leave?"

"Yes," Mosi says. Anika then drives over to her home. When she pulls up in front of her door she sees all of her clothing and furniture scattered across the grass. She has been evicted. She runs up to her door, turns the key, and the doorknob does not budge. She is locked out of her own apartment. Her knees reach the floor and she places her hands in front of her face to hide her dying tears. Mosi places her into the circle of his arms in a protective manner.

"It's going to be OK. I promise you. Please don't cry. I'm here for you." While holding Anika, Mosi calls a moving company. Fifteen minutes pass. The moving company arrives, picks up Anika's possessions, and delivers to Anika's mother's home.

"I've been evicted, Mom," Anika says.

"Why didn't you tell me you were having trouble paying your bills?" Ms. Muhammad says.

"I wasn't having trouble. I couldn't pay because I was in the hospital. I have nothing. I don't have a job or an apartment. I don't know what to do. It feels like I'm losing everything all at once," Anika says.

"That's how life works, honey. When it rains it pours.

That's why family is so important to have. No matter what happens, I will always be here for you. You will get through this. Thank you so much, Mosi, for being there for my daughter," Ms. Muhammad says.

"I will always be there for her. We do have some good news. We are getting married," Mosi says.

"Congratulations! I knew you were the right one for my daughter. So when is the big day?" Ms. Muhammad says.

"June of next year she will be my wife," Mosi says.

"Everything will work out," Ms. Muhammad says.

"I don't know what I'm going to do about a job. I've had the same job for a year," Anika says. Mosi hands Anika the Sunday newspaper.

"Don't worry; there are plenty of jobs. You will find one." Later the couple make their way to his apartment and Mosi is able to calm Anika's nerves.

The alarm clock rings at 10:00 a.m. the next morning, both of them awaken to the sound of relaxing music. Her fingers release the straps from the strawberry negligee she'd slipped on the night before. She lights lilac tea candles and places them across the front of the porcelain bath tub. The lukewarm water soothes each of her tightened muscles. She inhales as bubbles soften her now relaxed body. After her bath, she hears a knock at the door. "Yes?" no one answers. "Yessss?" Still nothing. Anika quickly puts a bathrobe on and her hair in a towel and looks through the peep-hole in the door. It's Mosi's apartment manager standing there with a judgmental look on her face.

"Hello," Anika says in a polite voice. The apartment manager, Susan, with a stern look in her eyes, hands Anika an eviction notice.

"You will have to vacate this apartment if you don't keep your kids from making noise outside of this apartment complex."

"We don't have any kids," Anika says.

"Several tenants have complained about your kids being in front of your apartment at night shooting off fireworks and playing loud music," Susan says.

Anika begins to raise her voice. "Wait a minute. I just told you I don't have any kids. This is not even my place. So I'm barely here!"

"I'm gonna leave this with you and—"

"No. I don't want it; you keep this," Anika says.

"You will—"

Anika cuts her off again. "No. I don't want it. You got the wrong person! Two apartments down those kids make noise all the time! You need to check with them!" Anika screams.

"Well, you need to report these things to management or you will be blamed. If you refuse to take this letter I still will be putting this in your file and—"

"No you will not. This is my boyfriend's apartment and he has no kids!" Anika says.

"You're gonna stop cutting me off and take this letter!" Susan says.

"Go ahead; put it in my file!" Anika says. They both turn their backs on each other simultaneously. Susan marches down the beaten steps and Anika parades back into the apartment and slams the door. Anika snatches her car keys and drives off to her mother's home to pick up some of her clothing. She unknowingly passes a police car spying behind an unseen bush. Still shook up from the incident at Mosi's apartment, she remains nervous and unsettled and accidentally runs two stop signs.

The police then creep up behind her as she's waiting at the red traffic light. When the light turns green she turns left. She is then blinded by a bright red and blue flashing lights. She slows and pulls over. A wave of tension chokes the air. The policeman treads up to her.

"Can I see your license and registration, please?"

"What's going on?" Anika asks as sweat drips down from her top hair line.

"Do you know why I pulled you over?" the policeman asks. "No," Anika replies.

"You passed two stop signs," the policeman says. Why didn't he stop me after the first stop sign? I could have killed someone, Anika thinks.

"Where do you live?" the policeman asks.

"I don't know the address," Anika says.

"Is this a stolen vehicle?" the policeman asks.

"Naw, this ain't stolen," Anika says disrespectfully. Another police car pulls up. A woman exits the car and steps over to the male policeman. As they are talking, anxiety creeps through Anika's veins. The policewoman heads for Anika with ID in hand. The tip of her dark shadow sails until it envelopes Anika.

"Can you give the address listed on your ID," the policewoman says. Anika looks up as she recites the correct address. The policewoman hands back the card and then the policeman returns.

"Here's your ID and registration," the policeman says. He then hands her a ticket. "I only put down that you ran one stop sign. Get your address corrected on your ID." She gives him a look of disgust as he walks away. Anika drives off.

CHAPTER 10 MOTHER-IN-LAW

The next afternoon Mosi gives Anika a call.

"I have a surprise for you. Be ready by twelve," Mosi says. He then picks her up and takes her to a popular lunch spot at Baywalk. When she first walks in she sees Mosi's mother along with the rest of his family sitting at a table.

"I want to introduce you to my family," Mosi says.

"Why didn't you tell me? I don't think I'm ready for this," Anika says. Mosi then walks her over to the table.

"Mom, this is the woman that I am marrying. Anika, this is my mom, Ms. Sultan, my brother Sadiki, and my sister, Kesha."

"We have already met," Ms. Sultan says, teeth clashing together.

"When did you all meet?" Mosi asks.

"In the hospital when you were sick. So this is the woman that you are planning on marrying. You both knew each other for eight years and I'm just now finding out about her. This makes no sense to me," Ms. Sultan says.

"I don't see anything wrong with it. He probably wanted to make sure she was the one before he introduced her to the family," Sadiki says.

"Well, I think I should have known sooner. So what do you see in my son? How do you know he is the one?" Ms. Sultan asks.

"I knew when I first meet him. We just belong together," Anika says.

"What do you do for a living?" Ms. Sultan asks.

"I don't work right now. But I am a student," Anika says.

"What do you mean you don't work right now? Mosi, you're marrying a woman that does not even have a career," Ms. Sultan says.

"I will have a career. I'm studying business and psychology," Anika says.

"What do you plan on doing with that degree?" Ms. Sultan asks.

"I don't know. I'm sure I'll find something," Anika says.

"You don't know. Why would you go to school if you don't have any goals for yourself? How long have you been in school?" Ms. Sultan asks.

"I think you're being too hard on her," Sadiki says.

"Shut up and mind your business. How long have you been in school?" Ms. Sultan says as ridicule springs off her tongue in an accelerated fashion.

"For a few years as a part-time student," Anika says.

"Well, my son has already graduated from college and already has a career," Ms. Sultan says.

"That's enough, Mom. What reason do you have to put Anika down?" Mosi says.

"I have reasons." Ms. Sultan pulls Mosi to the side. "Was she responsible for you getting sick? I feel she had something to do with it. Tell the truth," Ms. Sultan says.

"No, she had nothing to do with me falling into a coma," Mosi says.

"How did it happen? She refused to tell me," Ms. Sultan says.

"I really don't want to relive that day. I'm sorry," Mosi says.

"You're hiding something and I will get to the truth," Ms. Sultan says. They both walk back to the table.

"So what religion are you?" Ms. Sultan asks.

"I'm a Muslim," Anika says.

"You're a what?!" Ms. Sultan begins to choke on her food. Kesha passes her a cup of water.

"I'm a Muslim," Anika repeats herself.

"Explain to me how both of you intend on marrying each other when you have two different religions. What religion are you going to raise your children in? You all did not think of that, did you? My son is Baptist and he does not intend on being any other religion. Oh, I can't take this." Ms. Sultan walks over to the women's restroom. Kesha follows.

"He cannot marry this woman. What is the world coming to? I have a bad feeling about this woman. God help me," Ms. Sultan says.

"I think you're right. She seems stuck on herself. She's probably a gold digger. She's just out for Mosi's money. How can he marry a woman who does not even have a job? And who has a totally different religion than he does? Something is definitely not right with this picture," Kesha says.

"I'm not going back to Miami with you and Sadiki, I'm going to stay here for a while and look after my son. I'm going to make sure he doesn't marry this woman," Ms. Sultan says.

Ms. Sultan and Kesha walk back to the table. "I think it's time for us to go back to our hotel. I think I've heard enough for today."

"I think you're exaggerating, Mom," Sadiki says.

"Hush up, boy, and come on," Ms. Sultan says as she launches her right hand forward.

"Listen, Mosi, I will be staying with you for a few weeks so make sure your apartment is nice and clean for my arrival. Come on, Sadiki."

"It was nice to meet you. And I think you are a nice person. And a good match for my brother no matter what my mom thinks. I wish you two the best of luck," Sadiki says.

"Thank you, I really appreciate that," Anika says.

A few days pass and Mosi returning home from work sees his mother in front of the complex talking with the manager.

"What are you doing?" Mosi asks.

"I knew she had something to do with you falling into a coma. This young gentleman just told me that your future wife was there at the pool when you fell into a coma. So she had to see what happened to you." Mosi then seizes Ms. Sultan by the arm and lightly pushes her up the stairs.

"Come on, Mom, this is ridiculous; let's go upstairs," Mosi says.

"No, this is not ridiculous. You guys are hiding something from me," Ms. Sultan says.

"No one is hiding anything from you. Some things are just too painful to discuss; that's all," Mosi says.

"I do not want you to marry this woman. I get a strange feeling about her. I don't like her. Now I'm your mother. I raised you and what I say should go," Ms. Sultan says with uncontrollable rapid breaths.

"You really don't know her. Once you get to know her, I'm pretty sure you both will get along," Mosi says.

"I don't think so. Where is she from anyway? What are her parents like? How old is she? Do you truly love her? How can you be sure she is the one? What does she do for you?" Ms. Sultan says.

"I think after eight years, I should know for sure that she is the one," Mosi says.

"Why all of a sudden do you want to get married? I think this is a result of you going into a coma. You're not ready for marriage. You're only twenty---seven years old," Ms. Sultan says.

"You're right. After I fell into a coma, I realized that life is short and I have a good woman who I can share the rest of my life with. She is so beautiful and she is really good to me. She will do anything for me and I really think that she would be a good wife. I've known her for eight years and she has never changed and I don't think that she will. You have to trust me. I'm old enough now to make my own decisions. And I am ready for marriage and so is Anika. Please trust me."

"You're just a baby; what do you know about marriage?" Ms. Sultan says.

"I don't know a lot. I'm just going to take it day by day," Mosi says.

"So you all are trying to get married in a year. How do you plan to pull that off when she does not even have a job?" Ms. Sultan says.

"I'm sure she will find one. She's pretty responsible; she did manage to keep the same job for an entire year," Mosi says.

"Kesha thinks she's a gold digger," Ms. Sultan says.

"How can Kesha call anybody a gold digger? She is a gold digger herself. She doesn't work either. She has three baby-daddies and uses their child support to get her own nails and hair done, to buy her own self some clothes, and to take herself out to dinner. She spends little on her children. How pathetic is that?" Mosi says as he chuckles.

"Don't you talk about your own sister! What's gotten into you? This girl has really changed you," Ms. Sultan says.

"If anything she has made me a better person. I see life differently now. I'm just ready to settle down and start a family."

"You're making a big mistake. Trust me, you're going to regret this," Ms. Sultan says. Mosi turns his back and treads into his room to speak with Anika.

"So how is the job hunt going? Have you found anything that looks interesting enough to apply to?" Mosi asks.

"I've spotted a few customer service positions and a few counselor positions, but I don't think I qualify for the counselor positions," Anika says.

"You should apply anyway; you never know. We do have a wedding to plan so I hope you find something soon.," Mosi says.

"I know that. What's up with you?" Anika asks.

"Nothing. I just want to make sure we have enough money saved up. The wedding is only a year away and I figure with you and me working, we could save up at least five thousand dollars," Mosi says.

"We will, what got you worried all of a sudden," Anika says as her eyes give off a suspicious squint.

"I'm not worried. I just want to make sure you find a job," Mosi says.

"I will. You know you're acting pretty strange. Does this conversation have anything to do with your mother's influence?" Anika says.

"No it's not my mother." Mosi says. While Anika and Mosi are talking, Ms. Sultan is listening behind the door. Mosi opens the door and accidentally bumps into his mother. "What are you doing snooping?" Mosi asks.

"I'm not snooping. I was just walking by," Ms. Sultan says.

"This place is messy. Make sure you wash those dishes, vacuum this floor, and clean out this dirty closet. I want it all done by tonight! And the furniture needs rearranging. I don't like the way you have this place set up. You can do better. Help me move this couch," Ms. Sultan says.

"No, Mom. I plan on going to a party tonight. I'll straighten up tomorrow," Mosi says.

"Boy, you do as I say and clean this place up. I'm your mother," Ms. Sultan says as her face frowns up in a hideous appearance. Butterflies race throughout his stomach causing him to end the phone call with Anika.

"I'm not a kid anymore. This is my place and I set the rules," Mosi says.

"Oh, no, you're not going to a party tonight with this place looking like this. You stay and clean," Ms. Sultan says. And so Mosi does. He remains home all night cleaning and rearranging his furniture.

"I cannot believe how filthy this place is. I'm pretty sure his girlfriend comes over here a lot and does not even bother to clean up. A woman must be clean and keep a clean house in order to satisfy a man. That's another reason as to why she is not good for my son. She should have at least told him that his place was filthy. What type of woman is she?" Ms. Sultan says.

"Yeah, you're right," Kesha says.

"Don't you think that they are too young to get married? They both are only twenty---seven years old. I was thirty when I got married and started having kids. That's the right age to get married. At that time you're at least mature enough to raise kids properly. And I know I raised you kids right. Even though I had to raise you all myself after your father left me. I was still able to do a good job so I know what I'm talking about," Ms. Sultan says.

"Yeah, you're right," Kesha says.

"And I also raised you up to be Baptist. This girl is going to make my son change his religion. And I will just have a heart attack if that happens. You know your father changed his religion to Islam right before we separated. His whole personality changed; even the way he prayed changed. It scared me. Then he thought he could bring you children to church with him, but I would not allow that. He changed our last name. He changed your brother's first name behind my back. He tried to change your name, too. By then I had enough. I would not allow you children to grow up confused," Ms. Sultan says.

"You never told us that was the reason you two split up. I don't think a family should ever split up over religion," Kesha says.

"I knew what was best then and I know what's best now. I see the same thing happening to Mosi if he marries that girl and I just don't want that to happen. I don't want you kids to go through the same things that I had to go through. It's just too painful. I must convince him to leave her. It's for the best," Ms. Sultan says.

"Yeah, you're right," Kesha says.

"You and your brother's plane will be leaving in two hours. I'm going to take you to the airport so you better get ready."

CHAPTER 11 RELAPSE

The next day when Anika returns to Mosi's apartment, Mosi and Ms. Sultan are out at dinner. She walks in and drops her purse and keys down on his furniture and picks up a letter from his apartment manager and reads out loud.

"We will be checking all apartments consistently. Also everyone's guest is required to provide ID before entering this apartment complex. We have been getting a lot of complaints about loud music. Music is not to be played after 10:00 p.m."

"These people are going to be checking this apartment. For what? Are they out of their minds?" Anika mumbles. Paranoia strikes Anika's fatigued mind, causing her eyes to widen and appear glued to her face. She feels like she's going to lose her mind again.

"They're coming in to check this apartment. I bet the security guards have cameras up in here." She walks in the bathroom and stares into the small holes in Mosi's wall that were left by the paintings hung by the previous renters. She covers up the holes with toilet tissue.

"Those nosy security guards are not gonna see me while I'm in here. I need privacy. Those perverted security guards." After she uses the bathroom she removes the toilet tissue from the holes in the wall.

"I need to rest. I have not slept well in two days." She drives to the nearest store and purchases a bottle of wine. The cashier is a teenager and she sees a man pass by who is dressed in female garments. The cashier looks up at Anika with a smile of instigation.

"Did you see her? Is that a man or a woman? I think it's a man dressed up as a woman. He is a transvestite," the cashier says as she laughs.

"I don't know; I try not to judge people," Anika says. The cashier and the bagger look at each other and they burst out with unrestrained laughter.

"Your total is $5.15. Thank you for shopping with us," the cashier says. Anika hands the cashier six dollars and receives change back.

"Thank you," Anika says politely. Anika then returns to Mosi's house. She begins to pour herself some wine to help her sleep when she hears a knock at the door. It's Mosi's neighbor.

"You need to turn down your music. It's too loud," the neighbor says.

"Mind your own business; it's not even ten o'clock yet." Anika then rushes over to the radio and turns it up louder. She then runs to the peephole to see if the neighbor is still there. She sees the neighbor as she storms downstairs. She then runs and looks into the mirror at her reflection and begins laughing.

"I gotcha." Facing the mirror she begins dancing. She spins around and jumps up, all while laughing. She places a white glove over her right hand and crosses her hands behind her back as if she's going to jail. She begins to whisper.

"They better not lock him up. All that he has done for us." She then runs over to the closet. She throws Mosi's dirty and clean clothes everywhere to find her pajamas. She puts them on. She runs through the house in the shape of an infinity sign while tugging at the sewn---in weave in her permed hair.

"I want this out. I want this out. I wanna be myself. Let me be myself." She begins to cry. And with hands clutched to her face she drops on top of the couch and begins clicking her heels. She pulls her trembling knees towards her chest in an effort to stop the uncontrollable shakes.

"I want to be myself." She runs towards the mirror again as if she's going to run right into it. She then walks backwards, turns, and runs towards the mirror again. She turns her music up even louder. "I need to rest, I need to rest." Anika walks into her kitchen and takes two sleeping pills. She lays down for an hour tossing and turning, holding her head trying to shut out her racing thoughts. She whispers and began to ramble on to an uninterpretable extent.

"Atoms are neither created nor destroyed. There was always an existence. You have to take baby steps to understand how this existence works, where we came from, how it started. Don't jump from A to Z. No, you must go from A to C. Take a break. It has been painted. First there was nothing; it was blackness, pitch blackness. There was first the black hole. A plumber can understand the black hole. There was a white light. The creator is positive energy. We all have a little bit of positive energy. A person of positivity can change your life without saying a word. We try to increase positive energy which is the same as increasing spiritually. Once we are of that same positivity as the creator, we become one with him. Only a few souls have reached this seventh level of existence. The rest of us are growing spiritually so we can reach that level." It appears to Anika that she is making sense as she began to explain herself, justifying her words.

"Positive times positive equals positive. Negative times positive equals negative. Therefore, if you have any negativity in you, you cannot become one with positivity. The creator is all positive energy. Negative times negative equals positive. If you learn from loads of negativity you will learn from your mistakes and become all positive. It's mathematics.

Everything stems from mathematics. Less than a cup of wine is what I need to rest. Don't want to scare away this beautiful spirit controlling my thoughts. While holding the sides of her head trying to rid her racing thoughts, she runs into the kitchen and pours herself a cup of wine. Don't want to cause a bad interaction, two sleeping pills and a cup of wine. She begins pacing back and forth while massaging her head. Anika feels sick so she runs to her kitchen and drinks a bottle of water and grabs another. Must keep drinking. Keep drinking. Bad reaction from pills and wine. Must keep drinking water.

Must keep drinking. She continues to pace back and forth. As she sits, her knees began to flutter in a motion of panic; she feels numb. She feels she is going to fly away. She suddenly feels nauseous, runs to the bathroom and then throws up. Anika begins to question her mortality and finds it troubling. She stares at her reflection in the bathroom mirror. "I'm not dead. I'm not dead. I'm alive, but if I'm alive why is there no one around? Am I a ghost? Have I really died? Is this what it is like to die and become a ghost? Is this black shadow that I'm seeing in the right corner of my eye from the dark side?

Am I going to hell? I need to call someone but who? I don't want no one to think I'm crazy; who can I call?"

Anika remembers that she still has the prescription for Abilify that her doctor wrote when she had her first nervous breakdown. She runs into Mosi's room, knocks her papers off the top of the closet and searches for her prescription. She finds it and races towards her car for the nearest pharmacy. As Anika is driving, she sees five police cars; one following the other. Each car is painted a creamy white with the green strip of intimidation removed. She is so scared to admit she has a problem, but she has to build up the strength to ask for help. She calls her mother on the way to the pharmacy.

"Mom, I'm having racing thoughts. I feel like I'm going to have a nervous breakdown," Anika says.

"You know you can always call me. I won't judge you," Ms. Muhammad says.

"Please come by the pharmacy near Mosi's apartment; that's where I'll be." Anika finally pulls up to the pharmacy and rushes over to the pharmacy tech who is dressed in a white jacket.   She hands him her prescription, he looks at the prescription and he gives her a judgmental look like he's staring into the eyes of a lunatic.

"This prescription is expired. Is this the only prescription that you have?" the pharmacy tech asks.

"Yes," Anika replies.

The pharmacist sees she's in distress and walks out of the pharmacy to hold her hand. Tears rush from her scarlet red eyes.

"I've had a cup of wine and I'm afraid if I take medication the medication will cause a bad interaction," Anika says.

"Do you have a current prescription? When was the last time you saw a doctor?" the pharmacist asks.

"A while ago," Anika says. Ms. Muhammad then pulls up, crying tears of pain.

"Does she have a current prescription?" the pharmacist asks.

"No, I don't believe she does. It's been a while since she has seen a psychiatrist," Ms. Muhammad says.

"Why didn't you continue seeing your psychiatrist? This means you have not been taking your medication," Ms. Muhammad says.

"I didn't want to feel or admit that I am crazy. Only crazy people take medication. I tried the medication for a few days and then stopped. Admitting I have a problem is the hardest thing for me," Anika says.

"You're not crazy. A lot of my customers come in for psychotic medications. You are just mentally exhausted. You're a beautiful woman. You're not crazy. It's best to take medication so you can be yourself. No one is going to judge you. There's nothing wrong with taking medication. A lot of people have to take medication for the rest of their lives. People with high blood pressure, diabetics; a lot of people. Take your medication and you can feel normal again. Your daughter has been drinking wine so she cannot take medication at this time. Take her to the nearest emergency room and be sure they know of this," the pharmacist says.

CH 12 HOSPITALIZATION

Ms. Muhammad does as the pharmacist asks and takes her to the nearest hospital. Everyone in the hospital turns around and stares at Anika. She then begins to dance. She walks up to the mental health technician.

"May I have your social security number?" The technician says.

"888-88-8888," Anika says calmly.

"Please sign in." The nurse then begins to take Anika's blood pressure. Anika's mother walks after the security guards as they walk toward the security camera allowing Anika to follow the nurses dressed in calming blue garb towards the psychiatric ward. Two orderlies dressed in what she perceives as 'controlling nightmare black' come from the back and grab each one of her arms tightly. She thinks she has harmed someone and is going to jail.

She yells at the orderlies, "No!" The orderlies then stop in their tracks and they both give her a blank stare.

"No!" she screams again. She feels if she takes a step into the psychiatric ward she will be responsible for someone dying. A nurse's assistant dressed in a purple uniform walks up to her. Anika turns her head and asks, "Is it OK to go in?" "Yes," the nurse's assistant says. Anika then allows the orderlies to drag her into the psychiatric facilities. They lock her into a room that has an appearance of a small ivory box.

There's a strip of flowery wallpaper one foot below the white ceiling. The room only contains one bed and a camera above. The bed has railings on both sides and a restraint that is used to tie up clients who refuse injections. The room has no door knob; no way to escape. One of the male nurses points to the camera above and says, "It's not on, don't worry. You can change into this gown." Anika glances at him with steamed rage.

"Liar, I know this camera is on! You're just trying to see me undress." Her words reverberate throughout the closed-in room bouncing off the ivory walls with great momentum. Apprehension strikes him instantly and he turns to leave the room. The door locks behind him.

"What type of hospital is this? I can't even tell what color the fuckin' walls are! They're supposed to be white for us patients! White is a calming color, you idiots!" Anika screams. She then begins to dance. Her legs cross and she spins with great speed. Her wrists cross forming an X and she places her arms behind her back. She then stands on her toes as if she is a famous ballerina. Her fist then punctures the wall.

"Let me out of this jail!" she screams. She then sees a vision of Hitler and begins to march in place and salute towards the camera.

"I can love and forgive him. I may be his reincarnation and I'm of love." She then shoots a bird by raising her middle finger and screams, "Don't you judge me! I'm tired. I need to rest. I want to be with him. I can't help anymore. I've been helping souls for thousands of years, I need to rest now and be with him. I don't like that word help! It's time for everyone to take responsibility for their own actions."

Her fatigued body falls limply onto the bed and she rolls over three times.

"I can go back and forth as much as I want if I choose to," Anika says. She thinks of Mary who was abused by her boyfriend and she hugs her stomach and leans forward and begins to rock back and forth.

"It hurts so bad!" She picks up a piece of leaf that has fallen from her clothing and begins to shed tears of compassion.

"It's the small things that count," Anika says. She then looks into the camera and says, "I fear no one but—" She stops and begins to shiver as if she was frightened by someone. She looks to the right of her and covers her right eye.

"There's only one!" Anika says. She stops talking and shivers again. She grabs her lilac shoes and lies onto the bed. Then a doctor, one of the orderlies dressed in black, and a nurse barge in. She shakes the hand of the nurse.

"My name is Anika." She looks into the orderly's eyes with stern confidence. "My name is Anika." The orderly attempts to repeat Anika's name, but he pronounces it incorrectly.

"No," Anika replies.

"I need your assistance in giving me a shot." The doctor then gives her a shot and she falls onto the bed and instantly falls asleep. The entire time the male nurse and her mother are in the security room looking at everything that is happening.

Anika wakes up the next morning and she is in an unfamiliar place. She's in a different psychiatric ward. This ward is filthy. The sheets on Anika's bed smell of another client, the walls are smothered with dirt, the floors have not been mopped in months.

She walks out of the room and into the dining area. She passes other clients who are shuffling across the floor in a zombie-like state.

"Breakfast is ready," one of the mental health techs says. She then sits across from one of the elderly patients in a wheelchair.

"You know I'm God. God bumped me this morning. Read your Bible and you'll be fine. And your sins will be forgiven." Anika looks up at the client.

"Why do you think you're God?" Anika asks. The client looks at her with a confused look and then wheels over to another table. Another client sits in the empty seat across from Anika. This client is heavily medicated with psychotic drugs. Anika lifts up her head, looks at the client, and smiles.

"What's your name?" Anika asks.

"Christian," the client replies. Anika proceeds to eat while watching the client's every move. One of the techs walks up to Anika and says, "Make sure you eat all your food." The client then looks at Anika in confusion.

"Do you starve yourself?" Christian asks.

"No." Anika replies. The patient notices Anika is watching her every move so she makes sure she eats every bit of her food as to set a good example for Anika, and then leaves the table and goes into her room.

"Sexy girl. You look very sexy," one of the male elderly patients says.

"Come sit by me, sexy." Anika then gets up and sits at another table.

"Don't be shy, sexy. You're beautiful, don't you know you're beautiful," Todd, the client asks.

"That's enough, Mr. Lewis, eat your breakfast," one of the techs says. Anika finishes her breakfast and walks to her room. A doctor then enters her room and asks her a series of medical questions and leaves. A psychiatrist then enters and walks next to her bed. The psychiatrist is a Caucasian man who looks quite ill. He looks as if he is an alcoholic, as if he self-medicates, which is what a lot of psychiatrists and nurses in the mental health field do from what her friend Kris has taught her. "Are you hearing any voices or seeing things," the psychiatrist asks.

"No, I never was seeing things and hearing voices," Anika says.

"Then why are you here?" Dr. Morris asks.

"You tell me. I did not try to kill myself so why am I in here?" Anika says.

"Because you are at danger of hurting yourself or others," Dr. Morris says.
"I would never hurt myself nor anyone else. So why am I here?" Anika says.

"Do you remember having a relapse? Do you remember anything that happened from the time you left your home up until you were baker acted?" Dr. Morris asks.

"I remember everything and I never tried to kill myself. When will you let me out of here?" Anika says.

"We will see," Dr. Morris says.

"What is my diagnosis?" Anika asks.

"You are diagnosed with paranoid schizophrenia," Dr. Morris says.

"I do not have schizophrenia," Anika says. "Look at me. I'm attractive. I dress well. I act normal. No one has ever called me crazy before."

"Do you have anyone in your family that has a mental disorder?" Dr. Morris asks.

"Yes, my father and my grandmother," Anika says.

"If you have a history of mental illness in your family the chances are greater that you may develop a mental illness. Did you have a mental exam when you were eight years old? Your illness would not be as severe as it is right now if you would have been treated at an early age," Dr. Morris asks.

"No, I've had physical exams, many of them, but never a mental exam. I did not know there was such a thing." Anika says.

"Do you get headaches often, or migraines, muscle aches, shortness of breath?" Mr. Morris asks.

"Yes, I do. Especially headaches," Anika says.

"Do you ever feel paranoid or scared about anything?" Dr. Morris asks.

"I sometimes think my boyfriend is cheating on me," Anika says.

"Do you sometimes have a hard time knowing what is real and what is not? Do you hallucinate?" Mr. Morris asks.

"Yes. I saw a ghost before. And once, I saw a face in the clouds. And sometimes I see faces in my rug and on my bed sheets," Anika says.

"Do you ever feel confused or have a hard time making decisions?" Dr. Morris asks.

"Yes," Anika replies.

"Do you ever act nervous and have a hard time communicating with others?" Dr. Morris asks.

"Yes all the time," Anika says.

"Are you susceptible to stress?" Dr. Morris asks. "Yes," Anika replies.

"The first signs of schizophrenia may show up between the ages of fifteen to thirty-four. What age were you when had your first episode?" Dr. Morris asks.

"I was twenty-six when I first had a breakdown," Anika says.

"Was it right after a very stressful event or right after you started your professional career?" Dr. Morris says.

"Yes, yes it was," Anika says.

"With medication these symptoms can disappear. Would you like that?" Dr. Morris asks.

"Yes I would. Maybe I do have schizophrenia," Anika says.

"Acknowledging that you have a problem is the first step to recovery. Take your medication," Dr. Morris says.

"But what about the side effects? When I took medication before I had dry mouth, and I was always so sleepy. I would sleep all day," Anika says.

"Some medications are best to take at bedtime. And a lot of symptoms usually disappear within two weeks. If not, I can prescribe different medication for you. Just let me know," Dr. Morris says and then exits the room. Anika then goes to phone Mosi. His mother answers.

"Is Mosi there?" Anika asks.

"May I ask whose calling?" Ms. Sultan asks.

"This is Anika. Is Mosi there?" Anika says. Ms. Sultan says not a word and then puts the phone down and enters Mosi's room announcing with an irate voice that he has a call. She follows behind him to be nosy.

"Mosi, I'm in a crisis unit. I had another breakdown. Can you please come see me during visiting hours. I'm scared to be here. The technicians check our room every fifteen minutes and I'm afraid I may get raped," Anika says breathing rapidly.

"The crisis unit? Oh no, not again. I'm so sorry. I'll come see you," Mosi says and hangs up the phone.

"Again? Again? You mean to tell me you're marrying a lunatic that has been hospitalized several times in a crisis unit. Are you out of your mind, boy? A lunatic will not be a part of this family. Not if I can help it. You are not marrying this girl!" Ms. Sultan says.

"I am marrying her and I don't want to argue," Mosi says.

Mosi and Ms. Sultan drive to visit Anika, arguing about Anika all the way there. When Mosi sees Anika, he runs up to give her a protective embrace. To Anika, it appeared as if he is running in slow motion taking an eternity to reach her. He then sweeps her into his shielded arms and her head sinks into his muscular chest. Ms. Sultan walks up and stands next to them.

"We've never had a problem like this in our family," Ms. Sultan says.

"Tell me what do you think caused you to have a mental break down?" Mosi asks.

"I should have noticed the signs. I was having a hard time sleeping. I was really stressed, I had short-term memory problems and panic attacks where I could not breathe and I was shaking," Anika says.

"What is your diagnosis?" Mosi asks.

"I don't have a disorder. I had a nervous breakdown," Anika says.

"But, Anika, you know you have a family history of mental illness. Your father and grandmother are schizophrenic. That means you have a high chance of inheriting the same disease. You will not get better if you don't first admit you have a problem. Why didn't you take the medication that was prescribed to you by your previous psychiatrist? You would not have had a relapse if you would have taken medication," Mosi says in a whisper.

"Don't you scold me! I know more about mental illness than you do. I know that it's a possibility that I may have a chemical imbalance! I just don't want to be called crazy. Once I start taking medication that means I'm admitting to be a lunatic!" Anika whispers.

"Don't you get at my son!" Ms. Sultan says.

"It's OK, Mom. Stay out of this please. You're going to make matters worse," Mosi says.

"I think I want to be alone. I don't need my own fiancé to call me crazy." Anika then stands up erect as if she's going to leave. Mosi and Ms. Sultan then stand.

"That's fine. I'm not trying to hurt you. I want you to get better. I will leave if that's what you want. But I'll be back." Mosi and Ms. Sultan walk out.

CHAPTER 13 GROUP THERAPY

"Group time, group time," the social worker yells out. There stands a five-foot, elderly woman with chalk in hand. The clients walk sluggishly down the hall and into the meeting room.

"Please everyone sign in," Mrs. Martin says.

"Let's all hold hands and start this session off with a prayer. God, grant me the serenity to accept the things I cannot change, the courage to change the things I can, and the wisdom to know the difference. Living one day at a time, enjoying one moment at a time, accepting hardship as a pathway to peace, taking as Jesus did this sinful world as it is, not as I would have it, trusting that you will make all things right if I surrender to your will, so that I may be reasonably happy in this life and supremely happy with you in the next," Mrs. Martin says. She then walks up to the board and draws two large circles.

"Please everyone, name off things that consume a large part of your day." The clients begin to yell out. "Drugs, dance, food, fishing, stress, alcohol, women, work."

"Does anyone want to explain why they chose their word?" Mrs. Martin asks. One of the clients raises his hand.

"Yes, Charles," Mrs. Martin says.

"I picked drugs because I'm addicted. The reason I got baker acted is because I was at the club and a guy wanted to fight me and I didn't want to hurt him so I kept popping pills. I went home and that's when I passed out. My dad found me and brought me here," Charles says.

"How do you think you could have solved the problem in a better way?" One of the other clients then shouts out, "He could have walked away—" Another client then interrupts, "No, he couldn't; that would have made him a coward."

"What's your suggestion then, what do you think he could have done, Dan?" Mrs. Martin asks.

"He could have knocked him out. That's what I would have done; then he would not have ended up in this hospital," Dan says.

"What do you think would have happened as a result of you knocking him out?" Mrs. Martin asks.

"He would have went to the hospital instead of me," Dan says as he laughs.

"What do you think you could have done, Charles, so that no one would have ended up in a hospital?" Mr. Martin asks.

"I could have called the police," Charles says.

"That's good, when faced with confrontation it's always best to find peaceful solutions to solve your problems. Violence only augments violence. Does anyone else want to share with us why they were baker acted?" Mrs. Martin asks. Silence filled the room bringing unease to Mrs. Martin.

"How about you, Anika? Why are you here?" Mrs. Martin asks.

"I'd rather not talk about it," Anika says.

"That is fine, but may I ask why so I know why you choose to put up a wall?" Mrs. Martin asks.

"I've learned not to talk about tragedy because some people may be drama stricken and may cause me to dwell on the negative which will later depress me. I have learned that everything I go through is for a reason.

If the reason is not obvious, I'll create a reason. Telling everyone why I'm here will only cause others to pity me and I will never pity myself so I will never allow another to pity me," Anika says.

Mrs. Martin is then silent with her head down. A full minute passes and no one says anything.

"Who chose the word stress?" Mrs. Martin asks in order to break the silence.

"I chose that word because my girlfriend is the reason I'm here," Douglas says.

"How can you blame your girlfriend? Shouldn't you take responsibility for your own actions?" Anika asks.

"That's true. We cannot blame others for our misfortunes. If you don't realize you have a problem with drugs and alcohol you will never get better," Mrs. Martin says.

"I don't have a problem with drugs or alcohol," Douglas says. "Then why are you here?" Mrs. Martin asks.

"I wrote a depressing letter and my girlfriend thought it was a suicide letter and she called the police," Douglas says.

"Why do you think she confused it with a suicide letter?" Mrs. Martin asks.

"Well, I did sound pretty hopeless, I will admit, but I did not try to kill myself," Douglas says.

"Neither did I," Charles says.

"Neither did I. I could not sleep so I kept taking my sleeping pills and several pills from my prescribed medication and then I started having racing thoughts so I took some more medication. Before I knew it, I had taken 47 pills," Katrina says.

"There is a very small percentage of clients that are baker acted who actually planned on committing suicide.

Usually we get patients here like you, Katrina, who just wanted to sleep or took drugs to numb the pains they may have been going through because of life's problems," Mrs. Martin says.

"Drugs and alcohol are never good to take when you're having problems in life. That's when you should be learning how to solve your problems so you can grow spiritually," Anika says.

"You're right, Anika, unfortunately the lifetime risk for a person with schizophrenia to become addicted to drugs or alcohol is almost 50%. Alcohol decreases the liver's ability to metabolize the medications that are prescribed to you by your doctors. So the medication doesn't do its job and you end up having another relapse and getting put into this place. Even smoking cigarettes can make your liver work faster, decreasing the effectiveness of your medications."

Anika then raises her hand. "I do have something that I do want to get off my chest. I'm tired of counselors, psychiatrists and mental health techs telling me that I need to take my medication. What's so important about taking medication? They act like my world is going to end if I don't take my medication."

"Do you care to share with the group what you have been diagnosed with?" Mr. Martin asks.

"No," Anika says quickly.

"Are you ashamed of your diagnosis?" Mrs. Martin asks.

"I don't believe the doctors are right. They see me for one to two minutes next to my bedside and they think they can diagnose me," Anika says.

"What you have to understand is that this hospital and any other treatment facility serve as a short-term crisis intervention treatment unit. The goal is to get you stabilized and then released.

If you do not agree with your diagnosis you can get a second opinion from another professional in outpatient therapy," Mrs. Martin says.

"I don't want to go to a psychiatrist because I don't want to give out all of my personal business. I believe that all the psychiatrist needs is to know the symptoms that I'm going through and they can then treat the symptoms. They don't need to know every traumatic thing that has happened in my past. That's just not necessary. It will bring up past pains," Anika says.

"If you don't feel comfortable giving personal information that is fine as long as you do give the symptoms and allow the doctor to treat the symptoms with medication. Some people need therapy and others can do fine without therapy. They're fine as long as they take their medication," Mrs. Martin says.

"Well, I don't feel I need medication. There is nothing wrong with me," Anika says.

"Then why are you here?" Mrs. Martin says. Anika is silent and then looks up at her with humiliation.

"I don't know," Anika says.

"The first step to recovery is admitting that you have a problem and asking yourself why is it you don't have faith in professionals that serve years in school in order to save lives like yours. It only takes three seconds of your day to take medication. Three seconds out of 43,200 seconds of your entire day. Come on, that's nothing," Mrs. Martin says.

"I don't want anyone to judge me. I don't want anyone to call me crazy. I try my best not to judge others," Anika says.

"Well, I don't believe that. Everyone judges others," Mrs. Martin says.

"That's not true; some people do try not to judge others," Dan says.

"That's true. I try not to judge others. You can't tell if someone's wealthy by the car they drive or the clothes they wear. They may have five cars and they may drive the oldest car they have to keep from getting robbed in certain places. Sometimes I test people to see if they're judgmental. I wear my glasses and my cheap clothes, and put my hair up to see how they will treat me when they first meet me. Then I'll let my hair down change to better clothes and put in my contacts and do my makeup the next day just to see their reaction. It's quite fun for me. Some religious people think they are better than you just because they know every word in the Bible. But they never try to live a better life. They don't understand that the purpose of the Bible and religion is to make you a better person and to bring you closer to God. You take a step towards God he will take three steps toward you. So I love to test people. To see if they're judgmental," Anika says.

"Well, that's not right," Katrina says.

"What's not right? I'm doing nothing wrong. I dress how I feel. Sometimes I just want to be laid back and other times I want to be high maintenance. I'm just being myself," Anika says. "Yeah, she's just being herself," Dan says.

"Let's talk about medication again," Mrs. Martin says. "It's been shown that for many disorders, medication is prescribed in order to correct a chemical imbalance in the brain. Let's start with anxiety. If you have ever had a SPECT scan performed and you have anxiety, the SPECT scan will show an increased activity in the right basal ganglia.

The book, "Change your Brain Change your Life," by Daniel G. Amen, M.D., says with ADD during concentration the front of the brain completely shuts down. With depression, the deep limbic system is overactive and problems which would account for moodiness, irritability, clinical depression, increased negative thinking, negative perception of events, decreased motivation, a flood of negative emotions, appetite and sleep problems, decreased or increased sexual responsiveness and social isolation, to name a few occurs. He says with schizophrenia, the prefrontal cortex activity decreases in response to an intellectual challenge. Problems with the prefrontal cortex can cause short attention span, impulse control problems, hyperactivity, disorganization, And procrastination, unavailability of emotions, misperceptions, poor judgment, trouble learning from experience, short term memory, and social and test anxiety.

A few examples as to why you should take your mediation are that you may have a brain disorder; not a mental disorder. You're not crazy. Do you steal or kill others? If no then why would you think you're crazy? There is really something wrong going on in your brain. If you have any of these disorders, it's very important to take your medications daily and on time. It takes three to six months to correct this brain disorder and without medication the brain can become imbalanced again causing you to have a relapse. This is very serious. You must take your medication or you'll never get well. Your condition will worsen. If you think what you're going through now is scary and horrific wait until ten years down the line after several relapses and see how scary your condition will be then. Have faith in these doctors. They want to see you doing well."

"Not all doctors. Some doctors think they are God. They get a high from controlling others, but what they don't realize is that every time you control someone you take a piece of yourself away. And you end up in a place like this. I used to be very controlling until I realized that it made me sick and depressed," Anika says.

"I heard a patient getting beaten last night by one of the staff. He kept yelling, help, help," Dan says.

"I did too he was yelling very loudly," Charles says.

"That patient could have been in restraints and could have been hitting himself, but I'll look into it for you. And I do agree that some doctors are quite controlling. I remember one psychiatrist who was a former coworker of mine saying he does counseling because it makes him feel better to know the lives of others are more messed up than his own. A lot of doctors themselves take psychotic medications and a lot of doctors get therapy on a weekly basis. You have to remember that neurotic disorders can become psychotic disorders if not treated. Medication treats these disorders so you can live a normal life. You are normal. You are not abnormal. You have a physical illness," Mrs. Martin says.

"Then why am I here? Why am I in this prison called a hospital? We're being punished for being sick. It's wrong; it's dead wrong," Anika says.

"Yeah you're right. It's wrong," Dan says.

"Yeah, they make us feel like we're crazy," Charles says.

"I'm realizing that it is some of our mental health professionals' fault for adding to the mental health stigma.

I'll admit now that I've been told I have schizophrenia. If you look in the textbook and look up the word schizophrenia, you'll see a confused ugly looking person as an example of schizophrenia. That sets an image in minds of professionals as to what the disease looks like. I'm attractive, alert, and happy and I love my life. I'm not what you see in those textbooks. I had to take a class in school called abnormal psychology. Who is normal? No one I know is normal. Either you have a physical disorder, a mental one, or both. I think we should put an end to those many labels: schizoid, depression, anxiety disorder, mood disorder, ADD, ODD, split personality disorder, borderline personality disorder. Labels tend to stick to a person throughout their lives. Why don't we just identify those disorders as different types of brain chemical dysfunctions?" Anika says.

"I do agree. Now since we have named those negative things that consume most of our day, let's choose some positive things that can replace the negative," Mrs. Martin says.
The clients begin to shout. "Money, dance, ice cream, food, sex, reading, going to the movies, playing basketball, children, love, friends."

"Those are good answers. Whenever you get the urge to do drugs or alcohol replace that urge with something active and positive," Mrs. Martin says.

"I just noticed something seriously wrong," Anika says.

"What's that," Mrs. Martin replies.

"No one mentioned God. We are living for God. Everything positive that I do is for God. How can any of you get through life without knowing that God truly loves you?" Anika says.

"I can answer that. It's because I bet most people truly do not believe there is a God. If you ask most people if they believe in God, they will say yes. But are they truly telling the truth? Do most people truly have a full 100% belief in God?" Charles says.

"No. Most people do not believe in what they can't see. If people will be honest, they will tell you that. Tell someone you're gonna be a millionaire and will donate most of your wealth to charity for God. They will laugh in your face," Dan says.

"I am God. God bumped me. He pushed me onto the floor this morning," one of the clients says. Everyone turns and looks without saying a word and then Dan continues to talk.

"I've been told by a psychiatrist that I have bipolar disorder because I feel like I have closeness with God and because I experience mania and depression often. Can you believe that? If you feel like you're close to God then you too can be diagnosed as having a disorder. It's crazy. You would hope that people have closeness with God. Maybe if more people were bipolar the crime rate would not be so high."

"I'm told I'm bipolar also and I'm told I talk too much," Katrina says.

"So that's what the psychiatrist told you? It can be to your benefit to be talkative. You're pretty funny also; you should be a comedian," Anika says.

"You actually think there's hope for me?" Katrina says.

"Of course there's hope for all of us. If we can work together to put an end to the stigma on mental illness then people won't be so afraid to get help.

I believe that you did not try to kill yourself. Look at your manicured fingernails. It's obvious you take care of yourself," Anika says.

"Yeah you're right. I feel I should not be in here. I don't deserve to be in here," Katrina says.

"None of us do. You're not crazy. You may be sick but you're not crazy. No one should be punished for being sick. Look at this place. It's closed in like a jail cell. There are bars against the door; bars like we're prisoners. Can you believe it? We're in the 2000's and there are bars against the door. We are all gathered in this prison like we are all lunatics. Yes, group therapy is beneficial for patients, but I think it should be done during out-patient therapy and with the patients' consent. In this hospital we should have our own separate rooms like normal sick people do in a normal hospital so we won't feel so alienated from the rest of the hospital. Maybe if we are treated like sick people with physical disorders, so many of us won't reject to medication. I would never hurt myself or anyone else and I'm sure the rest of you feel the same way," Anika says.

"You are right about that; a very small percent of people with mental disorders commit crimes. There is a large stigma placed on mental health. There's a lot of misconceptions. And people always fear what they don't understand," Mrs. Martin says.

"Look at this place; we are segregated from the rest of the hospital. Even when we take a break, we're walked over to this tiny corner at the end of the hospital. It's not fair. We should be treated like we have a physical disorder. Have our own TV's in our room. Get a chance to listen to our own music with a cordless radio for those who might be suicidal," Anika says.

"Yeah, the radio and TV can be stationary in one high spot just like they have in the rest of the hospital," Dan says.

"We should have longer visiting hours," Katrina says.

"We should have a video game system in here," Charles says.

"There should be flowers all around like a real hospital," Katrina says.

"There should be an exercise bike or a treadmill. That will help when I feel like I have to keep moving, which is a side effect from my medications," Douglas says.

"There should be a nice couch and a rocking chair," Anika says.

"There should be better food. We should have a choice of what we eat. We should be given menus," Christian says.

"We should be able to watch movies," Peter says.

"There should be counseling from the mental health techs all day. There should be musical therapy, dance therapy, and recreational therapy; more games, and a pool," Anika says.

"These things are good but a bit unrealistic," Mrs. Martin says.

"Why is it unrealistic? Why should these things be impossible? Our insurance pays good money for us to be here," Anika says.

"If the mental health staff continues to treat us like abnormal patients we will never get better. As long as clients that are suicidal are safe from hurting themselves, we should be given the same privileges as others who are in this hospital for physical disorders and then maybe people will begin to see that we are not walking crazy lunatics.

Those that act up should be placed in a facility like this. That will make them straighten up really quick. I bet you that," Anika says.

"You may have a point there. Well, the hour is up; we had a successful session today. You all have a nice day," Mrs. Martin says. Anika leaves the room and walks down the hall past Mr. Lewis.

"You're nothing but a black slut," Mr. Lewis says. Anika then stops in her tracks. She turns looks at him and says, "I forgive you for what you just said." One of the mental health techs hears this, and walks over to Mr. Lewis.

"That's it. You're going into isolation. You don't treat people like that," Jose says.

"No," Anika says, "let me talk to him." She then wheels Mr. Lewis's chair into the dining area and sits across from him.

"Are you a preacher?" he asks.

"No," Anika says.

"I abuse children," Mr. Lewis says underneath his shameful breath. Anika then slams her hand down onto the table.

"Stop it, stop abusing children." Anika says.

"I have to call my preacher. Can you help me?" Mr. Lewis asks.

"You can help yourself," Anika says. She then wheels him over to the telephone, locates his church's telephone number and tells him to dial. He then dials the number and begins to talk to his preacher. Jose then walks up to Anika.

"He disrespected you. Why are you forgiving him?" Jose asks.

"This man is in much pain because of his sins.

He's already suffering. Look at him. He's always asking for his preacher. I know Mr. Lewis is in pain. He confided in me because I listened and I did not judge him." Jose gives her a crazy look and then he walks away.

CHAPTER 14 PATIENTS' RIGHTS

The next morning Anika is awakened by the loud intercom coming from the nurse's station.

"Med call, med call," the nurse announces. She then lines up with the other clients. The nurse hands Anika her medication.

"Where's my iron? I'm anemic and I need my iron pills. That's why I had a nervous breakdown in the first place. Don't you know the body shuts down first and then the mind? That's why I'm in here. I haven't been taking my iron pills. What type of hospital is this?" Anika's voice is heard throughout the hospital.

"The doctor did not put in an order for iron pills so you will have to speak with him about this matter," the nurse says.

"Oh, I get it. Since this is a mental ward you all ignore my physical illness altogether," Anika says pressing her head back against her protracted neck. Anika then snatches the medication from the counter and tries to walk off.

"You must take your medication here," the nurse says. Anika then accidently drops one of her pills.

"I'm not giving you another pill," the nurse says in a nasty tone, nostrils pushed up in dislike. Anika then takes two hundred mgs of Seroquel and walks off. One of the clients, Christian, sees this and follows her into the activity room.

"The staff treats us really bad here. They treat us like we're crazy, like we're not normal," Christian says.

"Can I ask why you got baker acted?" Anika asks.

"I'm an alcoholic. I was drinking when I lost my mind. I was saying how great life was and singing out loud when my sister called the police. They came to my apartment and arrested me and brought me here. They told the staff that I tried to kill myself and I needed to be baker acted. I was saying that life was good. How could that be confused with wanting to kill myself," Christian says.

"You know our community is not educated in mental health. Once they label you as being crazy that label sticks with you for the rest of your life. Whether you have a drug problem or a brain chemical imbalance, to the community, you're just down-right crazy." Anika then sees her psychiatrist pass by to enter another client's room.

"My psychiatrist hasn't seen me yet today. I want to know when I'm going to get out of here," Anika says.

"I've been here for a month and I only have seen my doctor twice. What they usually do is send in a nurse practitioner to see you," Christian says.

"But that's not fair because it's the doctor who determines when you leave this place, not the nurse practitioner. How can the doctor come in and only see a few of his patients and then leave?" Anika asks.

"I guess the doctor has a busy schedule. I guess he doesn't have time to see every patient. Just be glad you're still here at the hospital. Most patients who don't have good insurance are shipped off to a tiny crisis unit where they see their doctors less than we do. At least you can stay here in this hospital.

Be thankful," Christian says.

Upset, Anika grabs her solution focused chart that she learned how to create from her friend Kris. The chart pinpoints what she needs to do to care of herself after discharge. She then marches into one of the clients' room where the doctor is sitting. "I have my solution focused chart developed, I'm writing in my journal, I've attended group therapy and I'm taking my medications. What else do I need to do to get out of here?" Anika says. The doctor does not say a word and leaves the room. Anika follows him, chart in hand. The other clients follow her. Since she's not getting anywhere using logic, she thought, she decides to rip up her chart and throws the paper alongside the hallway walls. She then runs into her room takes a piece of paper towel and begins wiping the filthy windows, walls, and floors.

"Clean this messy place!" Anika screams. She then runs back into the kitchen and grabs some ice. In her mind, she thinks by drinking the ice she will not go insane. She then begins to laugh and run across the floor in an infinity sign. "Clean up this mess, wash these floors," she begins singing in an opera voice. She then runs into the kitchen and pretends the table is a piano and begins pressing imaginary keys. The staff and clients look up in amazement. She then begins to dance like a professional ballerina dancer.

"Get me out of here, I'm not crazy," she begins to scream. She then runs up to the front desk.

"I want to see my chart, now. I want to know why I'm still here," Anika says.

"You are not able to see your chart, not until you are discharged. You can put in a petition for writ of habeas corpus if you want to leave this hospital," the nurse says.

The nurse then hands her a form to fill out.

"Don't fill that out. They will take you to court, and since everyone will think you're crazy, you'll never get out of here! Tear it up!" one of the clients shouts. All of the clients then begin to yell at the staff and tear up their forms. "Tear it up, Tear it up, Tear it up!" The clients begin to run around the crisis unit laughing. One of the clients in a wheel chair allows another client to turn him around until he's dizzy.

"You think we're crazy, we will act crazy. You treat us like we are abnormal, so we'll act that way," one of the clients yells out. Anika sits against the bathroom door. Her eyes peek up at the camera on the wall and she begins to brush her hair demonstrating that she is just as beautiful and normal as anyone else. She continues to bite down on the ice. Three of the clients race down the hall.

"Everyone, make up your beds. Crazy people don't make up their beds. Everyone, keep your room clean," Anika shouts as she leans up against the bathroom door. Two of the clients run for the exit door and begin tugging at the attached bars.

"Let us out of here," they shout. Three of the mental health technicians and one nurse then grab Anika and drag her into lockup. The techs hold her down. She fights to be released.

"I'll kick your fuckin' ass!" The nurse then gives Anika a shot that knocked her out. She's brought to the lockup room and promptly falls onto the rigid mat.Anika awakens four hours later and heads towards her room. Her psychiatrist is there waiting with her chart in hand.

"I'm aware that you had another relapse yesterday. Can you explain what caused you to relapse?" the doctor asks.

"You. You're the reason for my relapse. I see you maybe a few minutes a day. From those few minutes you can change my entire life, diagnosing me with schizophrenia and keeping me in this jail cell. I want out. I want out of this place now!" Anika says.

"You can leave today," the doctor says. There is then a moment of dead silence and the doctor repeats himself, "You can leave today." Anika cannot speak, she does not like being played with one bit and she will not be a part of this doctor's pranks.

"The social worker has found an outpatient psychiatrist and therapist for you. This is a short stabilization crisis unit. If you want a second opinion about your diagnosis then feel free. I will leave your prescription with you. If you do not take your medication and you are hospitalized again, I will have no choice but to commit you," the doctor says.

Anika, speechless, takes the prescription and remains sitting on her bed for a few minutes trying to suck in all that has happened to her. She phones Mosi and he arrives in a matter of minutes.

"Let's see your prescription," Mosi says. Anika hands over the prescription and Mosi looks over it as if he is a professional doctor.

"I am going to watch you take your medication each night. End of discussion," Mosi said.

CHAPTER 15 OBSESSION

Her exam is complete. She is so excited, she thinks of David. She forgets she had not spoken to him for over a month. David waits by the telephone daily for Anika's call. He calls her three times a day and never receives call back. This has caused much hurt for David and he is not afraid to make Anika aware of the pain she has caused.

"David I'm finished," Anika says.

"Who is this?" David asks.

"Oh, I'm sorry." He then recognizes Anika's voice.

"I have not spoken to you for over a month. Why do you do this to me?"

"I'm sorry," Anika says.

"Damn, woman. What did I do? Why didn't you call me?"

"I have something to tell you," Anika says. She knows she has to end things with David and she is terrified as to what David's reaction may be.

"What's that?" David asks. She then breathes in and then exhales.

"I can't continue to see you anymore," Anika says.

"What? What do you mean?" David asks.

"I'm getting married," Anika says. There is an uncomfortable silence.

"NO!" David's tears spring from his eyes in a rainstorm of helplessness. "Please don't do this to me. We were becoming so close," David says.

"But you knew I had someone," Anika says.

David's voice rings out in a psychotic roar, "I don't care! Why are you doing this to me?!"

Anika becomes a little frightened and begins to stutter.

"I...I'm sorry," Anika says.

"NO. Don't do this to me. I love you. You know I love you." He hangs up the phone. She then mumbles underneath her breath,

"Oh, I can't believe he just hung up on me." She is so distraught from that conversation she calls on her friend Mary. Mary answers, "Hello."

"Hey Mary, it's me. You won't believe what just happened to me."

"What," Mary says excitedly.

"The guy I've been seeing just hung up on me," Anika says. Mary is thrilled to welcome drama.

"I've been seeing this guy behind Mosi's back for a few months and he found out," Anika says.

"Was the relationship serious; did you have sex?" Mary asks.

"That's none of your business," Anika says, appalled that Mary can be so rude.

"Sorry. I was just asking, I wanta know everything. Don't leave out the juicy stuff," Mary says. Mary continues interrogating Anika for thirty minutes. Anika tries to change the conversation in order to keep her blood from boiling.

"So how is your relationship going? Did you stay with the guy that beat on you, or did you break up with him?" Anika questions.

"I'm still with him," Mary says.

"What!" Anika says, shocked that Mary could be so confused. Anika and Mary decide to see a movie to make their day go by faster. One hour later, Mary arrives at Anika's boyfriend's house. After the first knock Anika answers.

"So I see you're at your boyfriend's house a lot now," Mary says smirking slightly.

"No, not boyfriend, fiancé," Anika says.
Mary's eyes widen and give off a look of awe, "Fiancé, oh, my God, let me see that ring! Go ahead, girl. I can't believe it! How can you cheat on a man and then become engaged? You're gonna have to teach me this trick," Mary says.

"Real funny," Anika says.

"I want you to be my maid of honor," Anika says. Mary accepts with open arms. Mary and Anika leave the apartment for the movies. As they both step into Mary's car, Anika begins to feel unnerved as if she is being stalked. On the way to the mall where the theatre is located Anika continues to look out of Mary's rear view mirror. Thirty minutes later they arrive at the movie theater. Anika repeatedly looks behind her back as she saunters toward the theater. After the movie is over Mary drives Anika back to her boyfriend's home. The phone rings as soon as they both step into the apartment. Anika answers.

"Hello. Who is it?" Anika asks. No one is on the other line. "All right," Mary says, "you are really scarring me. I'm getting ready to go. Thank you for seeing the movie with—"

"Please don't leave," Anika says with a quivering voice.

"Oh, I'm sorry but I'm definitely leaving and besides, my man is probably waiting on me," Mary says.

As Mary paces toward the door, they both hear three knocks, jump back, and scream.

"Who is it?" Anika yells.

"It's me open the damn door!" Her boyfriend then enters. "What's going on?" Mosi says looking at them both with a stare of annoyance.

"Why are you guys screaming?" Mosi says.

"We thought you were someone else," Mary says.

"Who else were you expecting?" Mosi asks.

"No one," Anika answers hastily.

"Mary, weren't you just leaving?" Anika asks holding the door open and signaling with her right eye the way towards the much needed exodus. The phone rings again.

"Can you get that, baby?" Mosi says while keeping a curious eye on Anika. Anika pretends she does not hear him. He repeats himself. "Baby, can you get the phone please." She then answers the phone, walks into the bedroom, and shuts the door.

"Who is this?" Anika whispers.

"You know who the hell this is!" David says.

"Don't call here anymore," Anika says. She then hangs up the phone. David then calls her back.

"I told you not to call here anymore," Anika says. David's unwanted tone of voice hits up against her ears with abuse.

"Why are you doing this to me! You know I love you. I'm the one who taught you to love yourself, how can you do this to me?"

She hangs up the phone and saunters into the living room where Mosi is on the couch watching TV.

"Who was that?" Mosi asks.

"Oh, it was the wrong number," Anika says.

"Twice?" Mosi asks.

"Yes," Anika replies. The phone then rings again. Anika jumps.

"Please do not answer it. It's a wrong number," Anika says. The phone rings again.

"Who is this?" Mosi says suspiciously. The phone stops ringing. There is a knock at the door.

"Who is it?" Mosi asks in an angry voice. Anika then comes running out of the bedroom towards the front door.

"Who is it?" Mosi asks.

"I don't know," Anika says. Mosi then grabs for the doorknob. "Don't open it!" she screams.

"What's going on?" Mosi asks going with his gut telling him that his soon-to-be-wife is hiding something from him.

"I'm afraid," Anika says.

"Afraid of what?" Mosi asks.

"It might be him," Anika says.

"Him who?" Mosi says with great frustration. "David," Anika says.

"David! Don't tell me you haven't broken it off with him yet!" Mosi says.

"I have, but I don't think he is going to take no for an answer," Anika says.

"Oh, he better take no for an answer," Mosi says. He opens the door and walks around the apartment complex and sees a Caucasian young man standing outside with something in his hand. He thinks nothing of him and then treads back up stairs.

"Did you see anyone?" Anika apprehensively asks. "I only saw a white guy outside," Mosi says.

"Oh, shoot, how did he look?" Anika says.

"I don't know! Like a white guy!" Mosi says. "David is white!" Anika shouted.

"You were dating a white guy?" Mosi asks.

"Yes, and what's wrong with him being Caucasian?" Anika says.

"I can't believe you!" Mosi goes back outside and sees no one. He strolls back upstairs, "There's no one here—" He then sees the same man he saw outside, in his apartment with his hands smothered tightly around Anika's throat.

"It's David," she screams. Mosi charges David with his fist leading the way. David's face flies causing his grip around Anika's neck to weaken and his body to fall to the floor. As David drops onto the floor head first, Mosi begins lashing out at him, kicking every limb on David's bruised body. Petrified, Anika then races for the telephone and dials the police. The police arrive, arrest David and send him to jail. The next day Mary gives Anika a call begging to borrow money to bail her boyfriend out of jail.

Both Mosi and Anika are astounded by the coincidence.

CHAPTER 16 PROFESSOR

Hours later, Anika realizes she has her exam to turn in that has not yet been edited. She gives a copy to her boyfriend to read and she keeps a copy for herself.

"There are a lot of grammar mistakes. It's going to take you hours to correct this before it's turned in," Mosi says. She looks over her copy again.

"Yeah, you're right. What time is it?" Anika asks.

"Its 5:00 and you have already missed your Economics class," Mosi says.

"Oh, that class. I forgot to tell you I dropped out," Anika says. "You dropped out? Why?" Mosi asks.

"It was too damn difficult. You know, they had the top business professor in the nation teaching that class. He even wrote his own books," Anika says.

"So why are you using that as an excuse? You're better than that," Mosi says.

"Yeah; you're right." She puts her head down.

"I should have worked harder. So are you going to help me?" Anika says.

"Help you do what?" Mosi asks.

"Finish editing this paper, retarded," Anika replies.

"Yeah," Mosi says. They both edit the paper together. When she finally makes it to class, class is over and the professor is upset. The professor actually shows anger for the first time.

"You're late, and class is over," Mrs. Kadeem says. Anika tries to hand the exam to the professor.

"Class is over; exams were to be turned in by end of class today."

"But what happened was that my boyfriend went into a coma, I got sick, this crazy guy is—"

"You cannot use excuses for your faults; you must learn to take responsibility for your own mistakes." She then looks up and looks into the professor's eyes.

"What?" Anika says.

"I do not and did not want to hear your reasons for not getting here on time. Sometimes I know without asking," Mrs. Kadeem says.

"What do you mean?" Anika says.

"You have missed several classes. You have missed several of my classes, and also several days in your Economics class," Mrs. Kadeem says.

"How do you know?" Anika says.

"Reputation. You are developing a bad reputation. People talk and your reputation precedes you. Be careful. Word travels faster than you do," Mrs. Kadeem says.

"Word?" Anika says with a confused look in her eyes.

"Yes. I'm speaking about gossip. You have been turning papers in late, coming in late to class, and rushing off before class is over for the past two months. It always seems as if you're rushing. And when people rush they are showing a lack of patience and a lack of control over themselves. Never rush. Listen. I will not accept this exam," Mrs. Kadeem says.

"No. I worked for a week on this exam," Anika says.

"Some have worked months," Mrs. Kadeem says.

"Please. I must graduate from this class; is there anything that I can do?" Anika says. The professor pauses, walks into her office, sits down at her desk, and says, "OK. Come." Anika walks into the office.

"I have noticed that your writings have improved and I am excited to know how far you have gotten, so you have a choice. You can either edit all of these exams or you can fail the class."

"I can edit all exams, but wouldn't that take a long time?" Anika says.

"Yes, but it will teach you responsibility and I feel for the first time you can compare your writings to other student writings and finally get an idea as to how good you are."

"But—"

"End of discussion. You'll need to be here each day and finish all of the editing by Thursday, which is the last day of class. Can you do that?" Mrs. Kadeem says.

"Yes," Anika replies. She grabs all thirty exams, storms out of the professor's office upset and calls upon her boyfriend. "Baby, you will not believe this."

"What's wrong?" Mosi answered.

"The professor is not accepting my exam," Anika says.

"What? We worked all day on that exam. Your professor is tough," Mosi says.

"Yeah, she is very unpredictable. She caught me off-guard. I thought that just because she was quiet and did not say much that she would let anything slide by, but I was wrong. She walks around like royalty; I guess that's why everyone treats her like she is a queen," Anika says.

"Yeah, most professors carry themselves in that way. So will you fail the class?" Mosi asks.

"No," Anika replies.

"So how are you going to pass without having turned in your exam?" Mosi asks.

"My professor is making me edit papers," Anika says.

"What?" Mosi says.

"Yes, I have to edit the papers for the entire class," Anika says.

"How many students are in your class?" Mosi asks.

"Thirty," Anika replies.

"You have to edit thirty papers? She is mean. What are you going to do?" Mosi asks.

"I'm going to edit the papers. What choice do I have? I'd rather do that than fail," Anika says.

"Well, look, I'm at work so I'll call you later," Mosi says.

"All right, talk to you later," Anika says. She drives home and begins to look over all essays. She is surprised to find that twenty-five out of the thirty papers needed a lot of correction. She thinks, I have been putting all of my time and energy editing my work and only a handful of students edited their papers; she was pissed. She realizes for the first time that she is a perfectionist. She misses class so that her work could be perfect. I guess this is what the professor was trying to say. This is why she did not have a need to look at my exam; she knew my paper would be on point. She begins to feel better about herself when comparing her work to others' work, she realized how great of a writer she has truly become. While at work, Mosi calls his mother. "I'm a little upset, Mom," Mosi says.

"What's bothering you?" Ms. Sultan asks.

"I think you may be right about Anika. A month has passed and she still has not found a job. She promised me that she would find one right away. And I just found out today that she has dropped one of her classes. She used to take her school work seriously. Now she's missing classes, showing up late to her classes, and dropping classes. I don't know what's gotten into her. I hope she is not seeing that guy again," Mosi says.

"What guy?" Ms. Sultan says tightening her grip on the phone, bringing the receiver closer to her ear in fear of missing important details.

"Oh, I didn't mean to mention him," Mosi says.

"What guy, you tell me what's going on. Is she cheating on you?"

"No, but she was seeing someone at one point and I'm afraid she may cheat again," Mosi says.

"I knew it! I knew something wasn't right about that girl. I told you getting married to her wasn't the right thing to do; at least not at this particular time. Maybe you all should wait," Ms. Sultan says.

"Wait until when?" Mosi asks.

"You have to be 100% sure that she is the one. Or else your marriage will not last. I don't want you to go through the same thing that I went through. Take time to make sure this girl is the one. Maybe you should postpone your marriage until she finds a job; at least that way you will know for sure she is not going to use you for your money. You know some women get married and then don't want to work and don't work. And their husbands have to slave night and day to bring home the bacon.

You don't want to be put in that situation, do you? There is nothing wrong with postponing your marriage," Ms. Sultan says.

"Yeah, I think you may be right. I'll discuss this with Anika over dinner tonight," Mosi says.

"Trust me, son, I have years of experience with marriage. I know what I am saying. This will be best. Postpone the marriage until you two get on your feet," Ms. Sultan says.
Later that night Mosi invites Anika over to dinner.

"So how is the job search going? Have you been getting any interviews?" Mosi asks.

"No, I've been sending out resumes but I haven't gotten any responses back from any of the employers," Anika says.

"I thought you would be able to find a job sooner than this."

"I thought so, too, but it's only been a month. It takes some people six months or more to find a job," Anika says.

"Well, I've been thinking that maybe we should postpone our marriage date until you find work. That way we will have enough money to save for our wedding," Mosi says.
Excruciating torment rips Anika's heart into pieces.

"I think that's a bad idea. Why are you so obsessed with me finding a job? You don't trust me?" Anika asks.

"No, it's not that. I just want to make sure we have enough saved, that's all," Mosi says.

"Who has influenced this decision? Was it your mom again?" Anika says.

"No, my mom does not control any decisions I make. I make my own decisions. I'm a grown man," Mosi says.

"Well, you're not acting like one. I'm not postponing our

marriage. We are getting married in June. Everything will be fine," Anika says.

"You're not expecting me to pay for the entire wedding are you?" Mosi asks.

"What gave you that idea? Did you speak to your mother today?" Anika asks.

"I did, but that has nothing to do with this decision," Mosi says.

"I think it does. You know your mother does not like me. She's hated me the first time she laid her eyes on me. I think she would be happy if this wedding did not happen," Anika says.

"That's not true, and don't you go on talking about my mother," Mosi says. Anika then gets up from the table and walks into the bedroom. Mosi follows her and wraps her into his opened chest and speaks softly into her ear.

"I'm sorry. Maybe you're right. Maybe my mother is influencing my decisions. I won't let it happen again," Mosi says.

CHAPTER 17 PHYSICAL ABUSE

The next day Mary calls Anika informing her that her beloved boyfriend has been released from jail and she has no idea who gave him the bail money. Anika drives over to Mary's house. After the fifth knock Mary finally answers.

"Mary what's wrong? You're crying?"

"My boyfriend, he beat me again," Mary says.

"What!" Anika says.

"Yes, he beat me," Mary says.

"What happened?"

Mary immediately begins to cover up for her boyfriend. "It was my fault," Mary says.

"How is that?" Anika asks.

"I didn't have dinner ready when he came home from work," Mary says.

"What? Are you serious? That's no reason to get abused. No reason is a good reason for abuse." Anika says.

"He does not abuse me. He just got a little upset, that's all. He does not mean to do what he does. And he always apologizes. He is really a good man. If only you knew him," Mary says. Anika then grabs Mary's bruised arm.

"You call this a little upset. It seems to me like a lion jumped on you," Anika says.

Mary then begins to scream. "Stop it, you're exaggerating. I told you he does not abuse me. He is very sorry for what he did, and it won't happen again," Mary says.

"Yeah, right. How do you know that?" Anika says.

"Imagine. If he can get this upset about food, what will happen if you ever screw over his money, or lie, or disappoint him in any way, and what is he doing living here?" Anika says.

"He needed a place to stay," Mary says. "What? Is he homeless?" Anika asks.

"No. He is a starving artist, and he just needed a place to crash for a little while. What's wrong with that?"

"I'll tell you what's wrong with that. He is a man. And a man should be responsible enough to have his own," Anika says.

"What about you?" Mary replies.

"What about me?" Anika says.

"You needed a place to stay and I allowed you to stay here," Mary says.

"That's different," Anika says.

"How is that different? You were homeless, too. You thought no one knew. I knew. I knew you lost your job. I knew you lost your apartment. And I said nothing," Mary says.
A pool of moist tears fills up in Anika's eyes.

"How did you know?" Anika says.

"Word travels. So you were not responsible either. You could not take care of yourself," Mary says.

"You cannot say that about me," Anika says.

"Well, you cannot say that about my man either," Mary says. Mary then pounces into her room and slams the door. Anika walks in after her. "I'm offended by how you're talking to me. I am only trying to help, and you know that." Mary is silent.

"I don't know why you always think I try to act like I'm an angel. I never claimed to be an angel." Mary remains silent.

"Yes, I am a perfectionist but I am no angel."

"You got that right," Mary says.

"At least I don't cheat," Mary says.

"I think you're taking this conversation the wrong way. I'm leaving," Anika says. Mary sits up from the edge of the bed.

"I'm sorry. Please stay." Mary begins to cry.

"I can't believe he did this to me. And all over some food, some damn food. I can't believe it," Mary says.

"It's going to be OK. Everything will be OK," Anika says. They then hear a knock at the door. Mary answers the door while Anika is still in the bedroom.

"What are you doing here?" Mary asks at a whisper.

"I am so sorry. Please let me come in so we can talk," Mike says.

"I have company," Mary says.

"Who is it? What's his name?" Mike says.

"It's one of my friends. Please leave," Mary says.

"No," Mike responds.

"Please, I don't want anyone else to get involved," Mary says. Mary's boyfriend then stares into Mary's eyes, walks backward and says, "I'm not done here." Anika then saunters up to the door.

"Who was that?" His voice sounds familiar."

"Oh, no one. It was a solicitor," Mary says. "Oh, OK," Anika says with suspicion.

"I know you probably love this guy and I can't tell you what to do. The only advice that I will give you is this. My mother always says if you are not happy, protected, and honest in a relationship then it may be time to move on. Never settle," Anika says.

"Yeah, I know you're right. And that's what I plan on doing, but I love him so much. It was love at first sight," Mary says.

"Well, you are an adult and I am pretty sure that as an adult you are capable of making your own decisions," Anika says.

"But you know how I am. I have this dependent personality. I feel like I can't make it without someone there by my side," Mary says.

"Well, I'm pretty sure that we all need someone to make it through each day but we must be careful whom we choose to be there for us. All I am saying is be careful," Anika says. Anika then exits the apartment with a look of bewilderment on her face. Anika knows something is not right. She has a gut feeling. While driving home Anika receives a call from her friend, the therapist.

"How are you doing?" Kris asks. "I'm doing fine," Anika replies.

"I called to tell you about a position that just opened up within the crisis unit. I think you would be a perfect candidate," Kris says.

"Oh, I would be embarrassed to show my face there again," Anika says.

"Why would you be embarrassed? You did nothing wrong while you were sick. As a matter of fact, you were praised after you left," Kris says.

"What do you mean?" Anika replies.

"After you left, there was a lot of talk about how your peaceful presence helped the other patients," Kris says.

"Oh, how did I do that?" Anika asks.

"Through your music and ability not to judge others. Once you began playing your music, the other patients began to request their music from their friends and family. After you left the clients wanted to play their own music and they started looking at each situation in a different light. They began to wake up out of their zombie state and because of that, their families began to treat them like human beings instead of sickly animals. Doctors and other staff members also began to treat them with more respect. There was finally peace through music. I guess you can call it music therapy," Kris says.

"And all of this occurred because of me?" Anika asks.

"Yes, because of you, your music and open acceptance. I took notice that the music that you were playing was very spiritual and also the music that you were singing. It surprised me because I did not think spirituality could be heard through rap, R&B, and soul music. It was a big surprise to everyone."

"Well, then," Anika says with an enthusiastic voice, "what are the qualifications?"

"Don't worry about the qualifications. I have already spoken to human resources; if you want the job, it's yours," Kris says.

"What would be some of my job responsibilities?" Anika asks.

"You would work as a community facilitator. It would be your job to ensure that all clients are linked up to the appropriate resources. Whether it is additional counseling, education, or financial support and to provide training on management of mental disorders in a group setting. I know you would be good at this job," Kris says.

"I think I will be too, and I want the type of job that will allow me to help people. How much does it pay?" Anika asks.

"I'm not sure of the pay, but I'm sure you know that in the field of helping others the pay is not too great," Kris says.

"Well, I'm sure it will pay better than I used to make," Anika says.

"Yes, that I can guarantee," Kris says.

"When would I start?" Anika asks.

"You can start immediately. Please give Mr. Rogers a call tomorrow. His number is 555-8268," Kris says.

"I sure will. Thank you so much!" Anika says.

Anika says her good-byes and continues to drive home. She is so excited, she puts in the CD that makes her the happiest and she begins to sing. "'I'm all woman now." After the sixth song, she has made it home. No need to knock and wait for him to open, she has the key. She is so excited from the news of her being a savior within the crisis unit. She begins to shout.

"Baby, baby, guess what!" She enters her bedroom. It's not him. It's David.

"Oh, God," she screams, "what are you doing here? How did you get in here?"

"I told you this ain't over. You can't love a man and then drop a man on his face. If you leave me, I'll kill you!" David says as his nails dig deep into his palms.

"I have already left you," Anika says chivalrously. The phone then rings. It's Mary. Anika picks up the phone while keeping her eye on David.

"Hey, how are you doing? I'm so scared I haven't heard from my boyfriend in a few hours. I'm afraid of what he might do," Mary says.

David hears the voice of Mary over the phone.

"Who is that? Is that Mary?" David says. Anika puts the phone down on the coffee table without hanging up.

"How do you know my friend Mary?" Anika says.

He then says in a creepy voice, "I know Mary, I know you. I know you both. How dumb can you be? I met you both at the same time." Anika then hears Mary crying and begins to walk over to the coffee table, turning her back to David. David grabs Anika's waist, pulls her toward his sweating chest and kisses her tense neck.

"You know you love me, don't you. Admit it." He grabs a pocketknife out of his pocket and places it against her neck and raises his voice in a controlling manner.

"Admit it. Admit it. You want me. I'll kill you. Admit it!" Anika reaches to twist his wrist and scolds him pretentiously.

"NO!"

He then backs up slowly, pocketknife in hand and begins to tear up. He stares into her eyes for a minute, says nothing, and then exits the apartment. She then runs for the phone while crying.

"Mary, are you still there?" She hears silence and hangs up the phone. She then calls Mary back.

"Mary," Anika says.

"Yes, it's me. I can't believe what's happening." Mary then gives an outcry of abashment.

"We're in love with the same man. What the?"

"Why didn't you tell me, why didn't you tell me?" Mary asks.

"I did not know. How was I supposed to figure it out when you lied to me?" Anika says. "How did I lie to you?"

"You did not tell me that your boyfriend was Caucasian. You acted startled when I told you that my boyfriend was a Caucasian man. If you would have told me I would have put two and two together," Anika says.

"Please, let's not argue over this. His race has nothing to do with this. His actions have everything to do with this, not his race. What happened after I hung up the phone? Did he hurt you?" Mary asks.

"Yes," Anika begins to cry once more.

"He put a knife to me."

"No! I'm so sorry. I wish I would have known this was the same guy. I would have been watching out for you," Mary says.

"I know, but now what do you think he may do next?" Anika asks.

"I don't know," Mary replies.

CHAPTER 18 OPPOSITIONAL DEFIANT DISORDER

Several months have passed. Anika must get ready for work. No need to rush anymore. She is now a professional salaried employee. She can go into work at any time as long as her clients are being seen. As long as she keeps her appointments and remains punctual. She loves this. She takes her time picking out the most professional suit she owns since she is preparing to make her first presentation at Highpoint Elementary. The topic of discussion, Oppositional Defiant Disorder. Since this is her first presentation that will be given to teachers and elementary staff, she is very nervous. She prepares herself by doing a thirty-minute exercise routine, a nice huge breakfast, and a long bubble bath. She is now ready. Her confidence is up. She prepares to drive; she puts in the CD that makes her feel the most powerful and begins to sing, "Yes I am independent, but I still need you. Yes I am independent, but I still love you. Yes I am independent, but I still cherish you."

Time then flashes by with a blink of an eye. She is now at Highpoint Elementary and is ready for her presentation. The principal of the school announces her. "I would like to introduce a young woman who has been working with families in a non-profit program. She is one of the hardest workers in the community and is here today to discuss a disorder that is not well-known amongst our population of professionals. She is here to discuss oppositional defiant disorder and its effect on elementary and high school students."

She then walks up to the podium and performs her speech.

"Good morning. Many are uniformed about ODD. It's a disorder that can be seen in children before and after puberty. You can diagnose a child with ODD if he exhibits several behavior symptoms consistently for three to six months or longer. The behaviors to look out for are frequent loss of temper, arguing with adults, actively defying or refusing to comply with adults' request or rules, deliberately annoying other students, blaming others for their own mistakes or misbehavior, acting touchy or annoyed by others, acting angry or resentful, and frequently being spiteful or vindictive. Are there any questions, at this point?"

One of the teachers in the crowd stands up and asks, "This disorder I never heard of, I thought bad kids were just bad kids, may I ask what causes ODD?"

She responds with confidence, "Oppositional defiant disorder appears to be more common in families in which at least one parent has a history of a mood disorder. It's also very common in families where child care is disrupted by a succession of different caregivers, or in families in which harsh, inconsistent, or neglectful child-rearing practices are common," Anika says. Another teacher asks, "What is the prevalence rates of ODD?"

"The prevalence rates range from 2% to 16%, depending on the nature of the population sample and methods of ascertainment. Meaning that this elementary may see one to five cases a year of ODD. It is important that a child who has ODD, or any other chemical brain disorder, take his or her medication on time, daily. I myself have been diagnosed with schizophrenia and if I do not take my medication, I will end up back in the hospital. Any more question?" No one answers.

The presentation continues and is wrapped up after each professional is satisfied with the answer Anika provides.

"You have done such a good job that everyone is speechless. Thank you for your time," the principal says. The presentation is over and she is ecstatic for she accomplished one of her biggest goals. She has been afraid of presenting in front of large groups in the past, but now she is so confident that she's prepared for any obstacles thrown her way. She now drives to one of her many clients' homes to complete a goal assessment.

"Hello, Ms. Hazley. How are you this morning?" Anika asks.

"Oh, I am not doing too great. I just received a call from my son's school. I must pick him up. He was sent to the office for throwing chairs at his teacher," Ms. Hazley says.

"But I was just out to the school ten minutes ago and I heard no such thing," Anika says.

"Yes, it just occurred. I am so upset, one of our goals was for him to refrain from throwing chairs at others and to refrain from throwing temper tantrums," Ms. Hazley says.

"Have you had a chance to take him to the non-profit agency that we discussed earlier?" Anika asks.

"No, not as of yet," Ms. Hazley says.

"Well, that's very important. We must find out what is causing this sudden outburst of violence. It could be a chemical imbalance," Anika says.

"Oh, I just don't know anymore. He's only ten years old. What am I supposed to do?" Ms. Hazley says.

"You only can take it one day at a time," Anika says.

"I'm sorry to end this meeting so soon, but I need to go out to the school and find out what's going on with my son.

Is it possible for you to go back out to the school with me?" Mrs. Hazley asks.

"Yes, of course," Anika replies. Ms. Hazley and Anika rush off to Highpoint Elementary. When they get there they see two security guards holding Ms. Hazley's son. She runs up to the security guards and asks, "What seems to be the problem?" The security guard looks at the mother of Chris and says, "Your son has been throwing chairs through the school." Ms. Hazley then shouts out, "Give me my son!" The security guard then releases her son and stands near.

"We must have him Baker Acted as soon as possible!" Anika says.

"I am not Baker Acting my son." Ms. Hazley takes the hand of her son and heads toward her car.

"I know that as soon as I drive off this behavior will stop," Ms. Hazley says.

"Please, you must have him at least seen by a professional," Anika pleaded.

"No." Mrs. Hazley begins to drive off while her son is still kicking the car door open. Ms. Hazley is so unaware of what she's doing. She almost runs over Anika, but the assistant principal comes out of the office and runs behind the car and grabs Anika. Ms. Hazley then drives off with her son screaming and kicking with the car door open.

"Oh my! That car almost hit you!" the assistant principal says.

"I know. Thank you," Anika says.

"Your job is definitely more difficult than mine," the principal says. Anika then walks up to the security guard.

"What caused all of this to occur?" Anika asks.

"I don't know. You would have to ask the teacher," the guard says. Anika then walks over to the teacher's office. "May I have a word with you," Anika says.

"Sure," the teacher replies.

"I am the counselor for Chris, and I understand that today he threw a severe temper tantrum and I was wondering if you could fill me in as to what actually took place from beginning to end."

"Yes, sure, no problem," the teacher says nervously.

"It started when he was at his desk quietly working on math. He must have become frustrated because he began knocking his math papers on to the floor. He then stood up and began kicking the desk. At that time I tried to calm him down by talking to him. That did not work so I called security. Before they got there, he left the room, walked down to the principal's office and began throwing chairs. At that point, the behavior specialist tried to step in and that's when Chris ran outside and the security guard had to hold him down. Nothing anyone could say or do would stop Chris. The behavior just got worse and worse," the teacher explained.

"What do you think is wrong with him?" the teacher asks.

"I really do not know myself. I am in the process of getting help for him, but I need more assistance from the mother," Anika explained.

"Well, good luck trying because I have been working with her for three months and I got no results from her. If you do get some type of treatment for him please let me know."

"I sure will," Anika says.

Anika is now more confused than she had ever been regarding any client. So she decides to drive to her office and ask the supervisor and therapist of the program for assistance. She noticed her supervisor in her car.

"Good morning, I just received a phone call from Highpoint Elementary. They were very impressed by your presentation. Great job," the supervisor says.

"Thank you. Before you drive off, I would like to speak with you and the therapist regarding one of my clients," Anika says.

"Sure. I'll tell you what, I will be back in three hours.We can all have a meeting then. Does that sound good?"

"Sounds good," Anika says.

Anika then goes into her office, types up her progress report, and waits for the meeting.

"I called this meeting today because of an incident that just occurred with one of my clients. He throws what many think are severe temper tantrums and throws desks and chairs when he is upset. I may need your assistance with this client," Anika says. The therapist then responds, "Oh, no. I think you will be fine working with this client yourself."

"But I think this child may be at risk of hurting himself and others and I am not qualified to work on this case by myself," Anika says. The supervisor then responds, "I think that you will be fine. All you need to do is focus more on working with the parent and not the client."

"But isn't it the client that needs the assistance more?" Anika says.

"Yes, but at this point this is all you can do, unless you decide to do therapy," the supervisor says.

"Oh, no, I will not be doing therapy," Anika says.

"Why not? Anyone can do therapy," the supervisor says.

"Yeah, that's right, anyone can do therapy, there's nothing to be afraid of," the therapist says.

"NO, I cannot and will not do therapy. I don't even have my bachelor's degree in psychology yet, and I do not plan on going to school to get a master's degree at any time," Anika says.

"Well, what are you going to do when the therapist is out sick or quits? Someone will have to do that work. Am I right?" the supervisor says.

"I agree, you would have to fill in for me, and the kid is already messed up. You can't possibly do more harm by administering incorrect treatment," the therapist says. Anika is now irate, for she knows that she does not even have a bachelor's degree and should not be working alone on a case of this severity. She thinks to herself, this therapist is nothing but lazy and wants to put all her work on me. I'm going to let God handle this one.

"Is there anything else that you would like to discuss?" the supervisor asks.

"No not at this time," Anika says.

"Well, then, this meeting is adjourned," the supervisor says. Anika then calls up her friend Kris and tells her how her supervisor and the therapist ganged up on her, refusing to assist her with a severe case.

"I am so sorry that you are going through the same thing that I had to go through. I thought by now that supervisor and that therapist would have stopped this type of emotional abuse on employees," Kris says.

"You mean to tell me that you had the same supervisor and coworker as I do?"

"Yes, I did. Remember I was telling you about me getting taken advantage of when all I had to do was say no," Kris says.

"Oh, so this is what you were talking about. I can't believe it has been years ago and they are still the same way. They have not learned from their mistakes," Anika says.

"You are right and believe me, this type of treatment on clients and emotional abuse occurs in several non-profit community mental health agencies," Kris says.

"But why do you think this occurs in so many agencies?" Anika asks.

"Well, one of the reasons is that the government gives out grants for these non-profit agencies. And to keep funding for a program, the directors must abide by certain criteria. For the program that you are in now, there is a criterion to see at least fifteen clients monthly or the program will be revoked. So in order to make that fifteen mark, the community facilitator and the therapist must do therapy, even though the community facilitator may not be qualified. The budget that our agency is working with does not allows the directors to hire two therapists."

"But this is not fair," Anika says.

"No it is not fair, but it happens every day, and it needs to be stopped," Kris says. Anika then pulls up to the apartment and sees her fiancé waiting with a bouquet of roses.

"How did your presentation go?" Mosi asks.

"Oh, you shouldn't have. These are so beautiful. You are so sweet to me," Anika says.

"So, how did it go? How was your big day?" Mosi asks.

"Everything went well. They loved it," Anika says.

"Well, that's just great. We should celebrate. Where do you want to go to eat?" Mosi asks.

"Dirty Birds Smokehouse."

"Dirty Birds Smokehouse, again," Mosi replies.

"Yes," Anika says.

"So Dirty Birds Smokehouse it is," Mosi says.

Hand in hand, they walk towards their car. They are so in love. It can be read all over their faces. At lunch she is quiet, he knows something is bothering her without asking.

"What else do you need to tell me about work?" Mosi asks.

"Nothing," Anika says.

"I can tell something is bothering you. It's that crazy supervisor again, isn't it? What did she do?" Mosi asks.

"You know I can't really talk about what goes on at work," Anika says.

"You must talk about it or you will explode. I'm sick of this. As long as you do not mention names you are not breaking confidentiality," Mosi says.

"Yeah, you're right. It's one of my clients; I think that he may have oppositional defiant disorder," Anika says.

"What's that?" Mosi asks.

"It's a disorder that's characterized by frequent loss of temper, arguing with adults, actively defying or refusing to comply with adults' request or rules, deliberately annoying other students, blaming others for their own mistakes or misbehavior."

"Wow that's a handful! I don't think I could work with a client who has all of those characteristics," Mosi says.

"He doesn't have to have all of them. If a client has four or more, he could possibly be diagnosed with having ODD," Anika says.

"Wow. How many people are working with you to help this poor kid?" Mosi asks.

"No one," Anika says.

"No one!" Mosi replies.

"Yes and that's the problem," Anika says.

"Oh, I think I've heard enough. You are a soldier for sticking it out this long. I would have quit long time ago," Mosi says.

"And I will when the time is right," Anika says.

"My God, I'm so sorry. What happened today that got you so down?" Mosi asks.

"A car almost hit me," Anika says. "What!" Mosi says.

"Yes, that's how safe this job is," Anika says sarcastically.

"How did you almost get hit by a car?" Mosi asks.

"It's a long story," Anika says.

"Well, give me a short version," Mosi says.

"I was trying to stop the parent from driving off with her son screaming and kicking the car door open," Anika says.

"By being a wonder woman?" Mosi says sarcastically.

"No," Anika replies.

"I've heard enough. This all sounds too crazy for me. Look, you cannot allow others to take advantage of you. Your only job is to refer those clients to the right programs, and that's it, nothing more. Repeat after me. My job is to work as a community facilitator, not a therapist," Mosi says.

"But the therapist takes over and does my job for me a lot of times," Anika says.

"Well, put her in her place. That's your job. Her job is to be a therapist and she should be just that, a therapist, not a community facilitator," Mosi says.

"Yeah, you're right. I do love what I do. I spent so much time working at my last job doing nothing but data entry when I could have been following my true path in life, which is what I'm doing now. Helping others. I have so much passion for what I'm doing," Anika says.

"Well, that's good because most people could not do what you do," Mosi says.

"Yes, but I'm not most people. I think I'm special," Anika says. "That you are," Mosi replies.

"All this talk about me. How are you doing?" Anika says.

"I'm doing fine," Mosi replies.

"I've noticed that you are having a lot of nightmares lately. What's going on?" Anika asks.

"Nothing. I'm not sure why I'm having nightmare," Mosi says.

"You never talk about this with me. When did the nightmares start?" Anika asks.

"I don't really know. I guess after the coma. I keep dreaming about your friend," Mosi says.

"My friend, wait a minute now," Anika says, while arching her neck back.

"No, it's nothing like what you're thinking. I keep having a recurring dream that Mary is crying and that Mary may die," Mosi says.

"Oh, that is scary," Anika says.

"Yes, I know. This is why I did not tell you. Is Mary going through anything traumatic?" Mosi asks. She then looks down for she knows the truth. She knew about the abusive relationship months ago. She knew that they were dating the same man.

"No, she is not going through anything traumatic now," Anika says.

"What do you mean now? What did she go through in the past?" Mosi asks.

"Nothing," Anika says.

"Come on." He begins to get frustrated.

"I know something happened. Something severe. Why else would I be having these nightmares?" Mosi says.

"Nothing happened. Would you just drop it?!" Anika says underneath her breath.

"Why do you always hide things?" Mosi asks.

"Because some things are confidential," Anika says.

"I'm sorry," Mosi says. Anika then gets up, goes into the bathroom, and calls Mary. She then walks back over to the table.

"What was that all about?" Mosi asks.

"What was what?" Anika says.

"I heard you call Mary," Mosi says.

"How could you hear me? I was in the restroom," Anika says.

"I don't know but I heard you call Mary. Just like when I was in the coma. I heard Mary crying," Mosi says.

"This makes no sense. How could you hear Mary crying while you're in a coma?" Anika says.

"I don't know. Maybe I was dreaming then also. Or maybe I have ESP," Mosi says.

177

He pauses and looks into her eyes. "I think you know something," Mosi says.

"No," Anika says.

"Yes you do. You must tell me," Mosi says. She puts her head down. And then she tells him, "David."

"What about David?" he asks nervously.

"Mary also knows David," Anika says.

"How does she know David?" he says angrily.

"Mary used to date him also," Anika says.

"What!" Mosi says.

"Yes. He used to physically and verbally abuse her," Anika says.

"NO," Mosi says.

"Yes. We were seeing the same man," Anika says.

"I think I've heard enough," Mosi says.

"I'm sorry," Anika says.

"So what now? What happened to David?" Mosi says.

"I don't know. I would have to ask Mary," Anika says.

"Well, let's call her right now," Mosi says.

"I just called her," Anika says.

"So. Let's call her right now." He then phones Mary.

"Mary, it's me," Mosi says.

"Yes, I know who this is. What's going on?" Mary asks.

"I need to ask you about David. You know—"

"Yes, I know everything. Anika just told me. David is out of my life. I haven't seen or heard from him for quite some time," Mary says.

"OK good," Mosi replies.

"What did she say?" Anika immediately asks as soon as he released the phone call.

"She says she hasn't heard from him. But I just don't know. I got this gut feeling that this is not over, that we will definitely see him again," Mosi says.

"I'm scared," Anika says.

CHAPTER 19 TELEKINESIS

Several months later Anika receives a call from the therapist she works with.

"You must come in to work early this morning. I just received a call from Highpoint Elementary, they have a student that they want to be admitted to our program as soon as possible."

"How old is this student?" Anika asks.

"He is eight years old," the therapist says.

"Why is there such an urgency to admit this student into the program?" Anika asks.

"He told his teacher that when he gets home he is going to kill himself," the therapist says.

"He is only eight years old. Do you think he is really in danger of hurting himself?"

"There is no telling. What I would like to do is schedule an intake and risk assessment appointment for today just to make sure. Please come in immediately. I am going to try to set the appointment for early this morning," the therapist says. She then showers, slips on her business clothes, kisses her fiancé goodbye and rushes to work. Upon arriving to work she's curious as to what steps have been taken toward getting the boy assessed.

"Have you set the appointment?" Anika says.

"Yes, I have, we must leave immediately," the therapist says. Both Anika and the therapist rush off to the home of eight-year-old, Brian Miller.

As they are walking up to the door, Brian is staring out through the peephole.

"The purple lady is here," Brian says.

"What's that you say?" Ms. Miller says.

"The purple lady is walking up towards the door," Brian says.

"Let me see. What are you talking about?" Ms. Miller pushes Brian to the side and looks out through the peephole.

"They are your counselors. Sit down on the couch and stop playing around with me," Ms. Miller says as she opens the door.

"How are you two doing this afternoon? I take it you're from the crisis center. What are your names?" Ms. Miller says. The therapist speaks first. "My name is Katherine Brown and this is—"

"That's the purple lady. Isn't she beautiful, Mama?" Brian says.

"Boy, shut your mouth. Please come in," Ms. Miller says. Both Anika and the therapist walk in and take a seat. They notice the house is messy. The dishes have not been washed, there are clothes on the floor, and there are roaches running across the living room table.

"Please make yourselves comfortable. I thank you all for coming so quickly," Ms. Miller says.

"You're welcome. Well, to get started, first I would like to tell you a little about our program, and if it's a good fit for you we can continue on with the intake. This is a three-month home-based program. I am a therapist and my co-worker is a community facilitator. I will be providing any counseling needed for the entire three-month period and she will provide any community resources that are needed. After the three-month period is over, if you are still in need of services, she will refer you to another agency. Does this sound like something that you would be interested in?" the therapist says.

"Yes, it does. He really does need it," Ms. Miller says.

"Please fill out these few forms. Brian, do you know why we're here?" the therapist asks. "Yes," Brian says.

"Why, why are we here?"

"Because I've been a bad boy," Brian says.

The therapist pauses.

"What do you mean by bad? What are some bad things that you do?" the therapist asks.

"The teacher doesn't like me. She says I throw pencils at the other students but I don't. The pencils move by themselves," Brian says.

"Do you think it's possible for a pencil to move by itself?" the therapist asks.

"Yes, it's not my fault." The lights within the chandelier up above begin to flicker.

"The teacher blames everything on me. She is a mean lady," Brian says.

"Why do you think the teacher would blame everything on you? Is there a reason she does not like you?"

"Because of things that I say," Brian says.

"What things do you say that may upset your teacher?"

"I told her I wanted to kill myself," Brian says.

"Have you ever had this thought before?"

"No," Brian says.

"Why did you say such a thing?"

"I'm tired of being different. I'm tired of being the weird one. No one likes me. Everyone hates me," Brian says as he clamps his forehead in shame.

"Does your mother hate you?" the therapist asks.

"No," Brian replies.

"Does your teacher hate you?" the therapist asks.

"No," Brian replies.

"Then everyone does not hate you." The therapist turns to Ms. Miller.

"Has anything occurred in the last few months that would cause him to feel like killing himself?"

"Nothing that I can think of. The kids in this neighborhood tease him a lot. They call him weirdo," Ms. Miller says.

"Why do they call you weirdo? You look perfectly fine to me," Anika says.

"I hear voices. The voices talk to me. They tell me things. I know about Mary," Brian says.

"Who is Mary?" the therapist says. Brian then looks up at Anika and does not speak a word.

"How long has your son been hearing voices, Ms. Miller?" the therapist asks.

"I don't know; this is the first of me hearing this. Why are you lying to these nice people, Brian? Tell the truth. That's the only way they can help you," Ms. Miller says. He begins to scream.

"I am telling the truth! I am telling the truth! I am not a liar!"

"What do the voices tell you, Brian?" Anika asks.

"Different stuff," Brian says.

"Do you want to hurt yourself?" the therapist asks.

"I just want the kids to stop picking on me," Brian says.

"Ms. Miller, do you have anything in the household that Brian could use to hurt himself? If you do, please lock those things up and you must watch over him for twenty-four hours to make sure he does not hurt himself," the therapist says.

"What do you think is wrong with my son?" Ms. Miller asks.

"It's too soon to know anything. But once a week for the next three months we will continue to provide counseling to find some answers," the therapist says.

"I think it would be a good idea for Brian to see a psychiatrist while he is undergoing treatment with us," Anika says.

"Where? Where can I take him?" Ms. Miller says.

"Here is a list of different non-profit agencies that provide mental health services. Please contact one of these services today. Also it probably would be best if he is put on medication," Anika says.

"My son does not need medication. He is not crazy," Ms. Miller says.

"Medication will help to stop the voices. And your son is not crazy," Anika says.

"So our next meeting will be for the same day, same time next week?"

"Yes, that will be fine. Thank you all for coming," Ms. Miller says. She and the therapist exit the apartment.

"That was a real weird one, wasn't it?" the therapist says.

"No, I think I may understand him and be able to help him," Anika says.

"OK, so now I guess you can continue seeing this student by yourself. You can handle it," the therapist says.

"No, this is another situation where I think we both need to work as a team. I had to drop Chris from the program since you would not help me. I'm not dropping Brian. He needs therapy and community facilitating," Anika says.

"No, I think you will be just fine by yourself," the therapist says.

"You will not get away with this. I am going to human resources. This is unethical," Anika says.

"Well, there's no need for that. If you need my help, I can definitely assist you," the therapist chuckles.

CHAPTER 20 WEDDING

Anika and Mosi snuggle up on his king size bed. There is a knock at his door. They both awaken and remain in bed. The doorknob turns. Suitcases are heard hitting the floor.

"Ah!" Anika screams.

"Why are you screaming like you've seen a ghost. It's just me," Ms. Sultan says. "This place is a mess. I'm going to be here for a few weeks to help you plan for the wedding. I've already made plans with a nearby preacher to officiate the wedding in his church. I've chosen the colors you will wear; brown and silver. I paid for a jazz band to play during the wedding. Also, I've seen your wedding list; it's too long. So I took it upon myself to call a few of your friends to uninvite them. I've picked out the most beautiful wedding dress for you, Anika, and don't worry, I'll make sure Mosi does not see it before the wedding," Ms. Sultan says.

"I've already picked out a wedding dress," Anika says as she looks at Mosi in disbelief.

"Nonsense, you have no taste in clothing. You will wear what I have picked out for you. I've also bought shoes to match your dress. I've spent way too much money to waste." Anika taps Mosi with the edge of her elbow.

"Stand up for me, will you," she whispers.

"I'm going to make myself comfortable. You two sleep," Ms. Sultan says.

Anika knows to expect the worst from Ms. Sultan, for she is never pleasant. She knows that she has tricks up her sleeves. Anika walks into the living room and sees Ms. Sultan folding an ugly wedding dress. There is gray lace on the sleeves. The dress itself is ivory instead of white. It isn't long and flowing. This dress would only fall to Anika's knees.

"I'm not wearing that," Anika says.

"Nonsense, child, I think I know what is best. You're not going to walk down the aisle in pure white like you're a virgin, are you? Come on now." Anika rolls her eyes and presses her palms against her temples.

"My wedding is a few weeks away. I don't have time for this. Mosi, please tell your mother to back down," Anika says. Silence creeps into the room. Both Anika and Ms. Sultan stare at Mosi.

"Mom, Anika is right. This is her wedding. She should do the planning by herself," Mosi says boldly.

"All the money I spent on planning this wedding and you're not going to be appreciative? I spent a lot of money," Ms. Sultan says.

"Come on, enough with the guilt trip," Mosi says. Ms. Sultan turns her back to Anika, walks into their bedroom and slams the door.

"I'll be sleeping in here. You two share the living room couch until the wedding!" Ms. Sultan says. For two weeks while visiting Mosi, Anika had to hold her tongue and empty the balled air from her fist. Ms. Sultan continued to nag until Anika vowed to stay away from her presence. A year has passed since Mosi proposed to Anika. It is now June 6, 2001, 6:00 p.m., a few minutes before the wedding is to begin.

They have grown close. They have finally bonded and feel as if they are already family. Only one obstacle stands in their way of marriage, the other man.

"I can't believe you are finally getting married. All these years and you two are getting married. And I thank you so much for making me the maid of honor. I feel so privileged," Mary says.

"You're welcome. You're going to be the next one getting married," Anika says.

"I hope so. I thought David was the one," Mary says.

"Don't feel too bad about that. Your knight in shining armor is on his way," Anika says.

"When you see a white horse, let me know," Mary says.

"I'm serious. There's no reason why you can't have the best. You made the right decision to leave David alone, and so you shall be blessed," Anika says.

"When, when am I going to be blessed? I don't feel I made the right decision. I feel like David needed help and instead of forgiving him for what he did to me and getting him help I left him all alone," Mary says.

"There was nothing you could have done to help him," Anika says.

"That's not true. I could have kept my distance, but still gotten him help," Mary says.

"If that's the way you feel," Anika says.

"Yes, that's the way I feel. I really did love him. He was the only man that I truly loved and I made the wrong decision," Mary says.

"Stop saying that. Any time you allow another to verbally or physically abuse you, then you do not love yourself," Anika says.

"What do you mean?" Mary says.

"If you love yourself and God, then you would not allow anyone to step into your boundaries and abuse you. You must know your worth. You are worth a whole lot and this is why you did not go back with him," Anika says.

"Yeah, you're right. But I do agree that it is good to forgive others," Mary says.

"Gosh, I'm so nervous. I'm about to get married. This is what I've been dreaming for my entire life and it really is happening," Anika says.

"Yeah, I think every woman dreams of her wedding day, except me. I know I'm not getting married," Mary says.

"Stop that. Yes you will. You will find the right one, once you gain more confidence in yourself," Anika says.

"Yeah, you're right," Mary says. Mary gives her a hug.

"Oh, I'm so happy for you. I'm so proud. You are really maturing. You're turning into a true adult," Mary says.

"I know. Ain't I, though," Anika says. They both begin to laugh.

Keys from the piano tap Anika's ears, and she prepares to walk the deck. The hall and deck are filled with gold flowers. Anika is covered with a flawless snow dress joined by a six-foot train that flows out into an overturned bouquet of ivory roses covering her shoes. Her black hair is in a twisted French roll. Her brother gives her away. And the ceremony begins. Her eyes are glued to Mosi's black tuxedo. His sideburns are neatly trimmed into a slight angle. His black pearl wingtip shoes shine as bright as her wedding ring.

"I have loved you from the first day I laid my eyes on you. You are my soul mate. I never have to wonder if you love me because you show it every day. You support my dreams and my goals in life. Whenever I need you, you're there. It feels like I've waited an eternity for this day. We've jumped over all the obstacles thrown in our way. And we're here in love, getting married. It's unbelievable," Anika says. Mosi then places Anika's palms in his hands.

"I promise to always love you. You make my heart smile. You're always there when I need you. You're my angel. I will never leave your side," Mosi says.

The reverend then speaks. "If there's anyone who objects to this union between this man and woman, speak now or forever hold your peace." Silence then fills the room. There's a tap on the window of the deck. The attention is taken away from the bride and groom and is diverted towards the cracked window. There's a figure of a man on the outside looking in through the window. Everyone is still. The preacher repeats himself. "If there is anyone who objects to this union speak now or forever hold your peace." The door to the deck opens and everyone curves their heads and looks.

It's David.

"I object. I object to this wedding," Everyone's eyes are wide open. David stands there in creaseless slacks, a dingy shirt with two buttons missing, white boxers peeking out of his pants. His hair hasn't been combed in days, and a trace of saliva runs down his sleeve.

Mosi looks at Anika. Anika looks at David and then at Mosi. David repeats himself. "I object to this wedding." Mosi then takes a step towards David. David takes a step towards Anika. Anika and David look into each other's eyes. The heart of Anika begins to beat.

"Tell me you don't love me and I'll walk away," David says. Anika looks into David's eyes.

"I love him; I love Mosi." The guests then gasp and continue to whisper. Mosi looks at Anika.

"Baby, talk to me; do you love this man? Mosi asked.

"I love you. I want to marry you," Anika says.

"You don't love me?" David sadly asks. David begins to shed a tear and then slowly walks out of the hall. Ms. Sultan walks up to Mosi.

"You're gonna regret this. I promise you that. You're gonna marry the wrong woman. See Kesha, you see what happens when no one listens to me. He should have taken my advice. He's going to live a miserable life," Ms. Sultan says. Sadiki grabs Ms. Sultan's hand.

"That's enough, Mom. Let's go home," Sadiki says.

And the reverend finally marries the two of them. "I now pronounce you man and wife; you may kiss the bride."

"This is so beautiful," she thinks as doves are released into the air. Anika looks at Mosi, Mosi looks at her, and they both begin to cry.

The sequel is now available! Buy it now or continue reading to get a sneak peak.

Shocked to discover her wedding never actually happened, Anika relapses into a chaotic world of inner turmoil. Can Anika reclaim her life and find the love she deserves?

CHAPTER 1

Anika gapes out of her narrow window with her eyes stretched to her earlobes, looking through the morning dew in her small town called Saint Petersburg. She watches as a small bee lands on the window seal. Her heightened nostrils saturate the aroma of rubicund roses. Her eyes are glued to the window as she visions her wedding day. Anika imagines herself covered with a flawless snow dress joined by a six-foot train that flows out into an overturned bouquet of ivory roses covering her shoes. Mosi's inquisitive eyes question why Anika keeps speaking of David? Anika raised her wide-eyes to find Mosi observing her.

"You keep saying David. Where is David?" Mosi asked. "He almost stopped our marriage," Anika said.

"Anika, are you ok?" Mosi questions Anika's bizarre behavior. She did not want to relinquish her visions. Mosi paces back and forth. The sweat from his bare feet moistens his eggshell carpet covered with the feel of rabbit fur.

"He caused you to hit your head on the pool," Anika responds as she gazes at Mosi.

"No, Anika, you caused me to hit my head on the pool because you wouldn't give me the phone. Anika have you been taking your medication?"

"Sometimes," Anika responds.

"What do you mean sometimes? You have to take your medicine every day," Mosi said.

"Sometimes I have to wake up early for work. I can't always take my medicine," Anika said.

"Where is David, Anika?" Mosi asked. "Why are you asking me weird questions?" Anika asked. Mosi ambles closer to Anika and places his hand on the top of her shoulder.

"Baby you have to talk to me," Mosi said.

"Didn't you confront David?" Anika questions.

"No Anika. The phone kept ringing and I heard static that day. I never heard David," Mosi replied.

"Didn't he almost stop our wedding?" Anika said.

"Anika, we're only engaged. We postponed our marriage until next year, remember?" Mosi said.

"I need to call Mary. She will explain everything." Mosi watches as Anika hastens over to the phone. He hits the floor with his eyes.

If you're ready for more, buy it now!

REFERENCES:

Daniel G. Amen, M.D. (1998). Change Your Brain Change Your Life.

New York, New York: Three Rivers Press.

Dr. Abram Hoffer, M.D. (2004) Healing Schizophrenia. Toronto, Ontario Canada:

CCNB Press Inc.

National Institute of Health

Sylvia Browne

The Other Side And Back

Blessings From The Other Side

Made in the USA
Middletown, DE
24 February 2022

61801819R00108